Below the Surface

John Hill

ISBN: 9781413788273

Printed in Canada by Printorium Bookworks / Island Blue, Victoria B.C.

Dedication:

To my wife Moira, and to my children, Jeannine, Paul, Andrea and Bruce, who have all sailed and surfed with me.

Acknowledgement:

I wish to acknowledge the fine scholarship of astronomer Dr. Hugh Ross and his excellent books which unravel the complex mysteries of creation and produce a symphony between Science and Genesis Chapter One.

Author's Preface

Fearsome beasts, especially predators, have always captured the attention and fired the imagination of the reading public. Among these creatures, none is quite as invasive of the senses as *Carcharodon carcharias*, the Great White Shark. Attacks on boats, bathers and surfers nearly always make top line stories in the media.

When the juxtaposition of an idyllic sail boat cruise is coupled with an attack by a Great White, and the fallout leads to the victims reassessing their own lives and issues, the story can cause the readers to rethink their own personal values. Aimed at both secular and Christian readers, the teaching content portrayed in 'discussions' between the astronomer atheist and the missionary helping him should stimulate fresh thinking about eternal matters.

1

Andrea Jensen loosened the draw-string to the hood of her light-weight windbreaker and shook her tousled blonde hair free as she stood up. Keeping the tiller of the Robson Thirty-two steady with her knee, she stretched and looked around her. Close by, off the starboard quarter, it came into view again, the gigantic dorsal fin of what she felt sure belonged to a Great White shark. It had appeared from just below the surface. The beast was keeping pace with the sloop but had seemed to Andrea to have come much closer. It was the fourth time it had surfaced during her watch that morning, although she was certain she had caught a glimpse of it the afternoon before, and had mentioned it to James.

She wondered whether she should awaken Barker and tell him about the shark. James had done duty on the dog-watch from two until six in the morning and was sleeping in. Ever since their self-steering gear had broken, the yacht needed to be steered or the tiller lashed. James preferred that the Robson be steered now that they had entered the Caroline Islands, north of New Guinea. Deciding to let him continue to rest, she fastened the ropes that James had arranged to keep the tiller firmly in place and clambered forward along the side decks and past the upturned dinghy on the cabin top.

By leaning out in front of the mast's forestay on the foredeck,

Andrea had an uncluttered vista of the horizon. Dead ahead she saw a small cluster of islands barely visible in the distance. According to the charts, these were either the Hall, or Truk clusters, and were about ten miles away. She felt a sudden surge of joy. They had made good progress since leaving Hawaii and this was their first landfall since then. Returning to the cockpit she unlashed the tiller and heard a splashing sound behind the boat. Looking back over the stern railing, she was startled to see the shark only yards from the yacht. Even in the ripples of the boat's wake, Andrea could clearly make out the huge animal's eyes which seemed to have focussed on her. The shark's dorsal fin stood about three feet clear of the sea and she estimated that the creature itself was not much shorter in length than the Robson. *But it was the eyes.* There was an intensity about their gaze which she found quite unnerving. Andrea felt that she was being considered in the same way a very hungry teenager considered which items to heap onto his plate from a brunch buffet table. The hatch to the cabin was open since the night air in these latitudes was quite mild, almost balmy. Stretching forward to maintain control of the tiller, she called out to James. "Honey, are you awake? You need to come and see something very scary!"

Barker rubbed his eyes and swung down from the bunk. He was clad only in a pair of shorts and he yawned as he mounted the steps to the cockpit. Squinting as he emerged into the bright sunlight, he was about to ask what it was that Andrea had seen when the boat lurched forward under an impact from behind. Both James and Andrea lost their balance and fell towards the stern. Andrea barely had time to raise an arm to ward off the lower stern railing that she was flung against. There was a sharp crack as her body sandwiched her left arm against the rail and a bolt of agony shot up into her shoulder. James heard her cry of pain just as he tumbled face down onto the cockpit floor, bruising his shins on the mainsheet traveller bridge near the entrance to the cabin. It took him a few moments to recover from the shock of the event and the pain in his legs. Then he scrambled to his feet and reached out a hand toward the girl. As his hand clasped her right elbow, the shark struck again. This time Andrea's head bumped the rail, and he lurched forward only just managing to steady himself by grabbing the tiller.

The Robson, which had been surging through the sea on a broad reach, suddenly swung sharply to port and the breeze caught the mainsail on the reverse side and the gibe followed. At this point, James Barker found himself unceremoniously dumped on the starboard seat of the cockpit, with Andrea thrown against him. Instinctively, he caught her and saw the anguish in her face as she held her left forearm in her right hand. As tears slipped down her cheeks, she gasped, "It's broken. I heard it snap!"

Out of the corner of Barker's eye he was just in time to see the massive head and open jaws of the monster shark as it nosed right up to the stern railing. It seemed to him that the beast was simply taking a good look to see where it might strike next. Then, it was gone.

"Quick, honey," he shouted, "You must go inside!" With an arm around her, he helped Andrea down the cabin steps and sat her on the saloon settee. "I'll be back," he said, and moved quickly to the locker above the chart table. Rummaging inside, he pulled out a Webley thirty-eight automatic and turned to the steps as the shark struck for the third time. The yacht bounced and lurched as though hit by a huge demolition ball. Fortunately Barker had hold of the hand-railing for the steps and did not lose his balance. Andrea, however, slumped over onto her side on the settee and lay there groaning.

Emerging into the cockpit Barker saw with horror the damage the huge animal had caused to the stern of the Robson. As his eyes took in the gaping hole in the counter stern of the yacht's hull, fortunately clear of the water, he felt the backstay which had been torn free, swipe his face as it swung loose across the boat. The stern railings were broken and twisted as if slammed by some gigantic hammer. Knowing that the mast was no longer being supported by the damaged backstay, Barker grabbed the tiller and swung the boat's bow around to face just off the breeze. This brought the foresail back into operation and the motion of the yacht settled down again. Remembering the shark, he looked around but there was no sign of the massive fish.

He reset the sails, and then grabbed the backstay as it swung near him. With one hand he felt in a side locker of the cockpit while keeping the tiller firm with has knee. His probing fingers found what he was searching for, and he brought out a length of woven Dacron rope. It was long for the job, but he was able to secure the loose stay to one remaining piece of broken stern guard-railing. While this would not give significant support to the mast, it would at least prevent the loose stay with its deck mounting still attached, from swinging around and damaging the sails or injuring anyone in the cockpit.

There was no further sign of the shark, so Barker lashed the tiller and hurried below to check on Andrea and her injuries. He found her lying where he had left her, and still cradling her left arm. Moving over to her, he noticed how white her face was.

"Honey," he said softly, "how are you? Is the pain very bad? Can I take a look?"

She nodded, and he gently removed her wind-breaker to see the arm. It was clearly broken, warm to the touch, and starting to swell.

"It's broken," he said, confirming her suspicions. She opened her eyes and looked at him, noticing for the first time the blood on the side of his face. "What happened to your face?" she whispered.

"Oh, it's nothing," he replied, then, "There is a lot of damage outside. That monster has taken a large chunk out of the stern and torn the backstay right out of its mountings. It has also ruined the stern guardrailings."

Andrea shook her head slowly and he caught the low "Wow!" that escaped from her lips.

"But *Skipping Stone* is basically sound for the moment," he told her. "I'm going to get on the radio and see where the nearest help is. Can I get you a blanket?"

She nodded and watched him as he handed her two aspirin tablets and a mug of water. When she had taken these, he placed her pillow under her head and spread a light rug over her. Then he bent down and kissed her on the mouth. "Love ya!" he whispered, "Just relax as best as you can, while I sort things out."

2

After checking to see that all was well outside, Barker switched on the power supply to his radio and tuned to a selected frequency. Then he began calling for the local US Coast Guard. Within minutes he was heard and he explained that a passenger had suffered a broken arm when a monster shark had attacked his sailboat. Giving his position as near to the Truk Islands, Barker was relieved to hear that there was a medical missionary on the largest of the Truk group. The alternative, said the radio operator, was for Barker to change course and sail on to Ponape, where there was a small hospitai.

Ponape was a fair distance away, so Barker decided to opt for Truk. He checked his charts and made a small change to *Skipping Stone's* course. Looking back into the saloon, he saw that Andrea was sleeping so he returned to the cockpit. Hours later, as the islands grew nearer, he became aware of a change in the motion of the waves. His charts showed shallower depths and the presence of numerous reefs surrounding most of the islands themselves. He knew he would have to exercise extreme care. But his charts were up to date, and he focussed his attention on the preparations needed to make a safe landfall. This entailed dropping all sail and proceeding under power. Moving quickly and expertly, he soon had both the main and foresail down and safely tied. Then, engaging the forward gears, with the Robson's diesel engine throbbing sweetly, he powered her down the clearly marked channel which led through the reef to the flat waters of a lagoon within. Finally he was alongside a long dock among a cluster of local sailing and fishing craft.

He finished tying *Skipping Stone's* bow and stern lines, and was examining the ugly hole caused by the shark, when a white-haired man dressed in shorts and a brightly coloured, loose fitting shirt, walked down the dock toward him. The American accent was a welcome sound in Barker's ears.

"Hi there! Welcome to Big Truk Island," said the stranger. Then he caught sight of the Robson's stern. "Oh, my!" he exclaimed, "However did that happen? That is *serious* damage!"

"Greetings," said Barker, "Yes, we were attacked by a Great White shark early this morning. The monster had been following us for a while and must have thought we would be good to eat. However, my main problem is that my partner, Andrea, suffered a broken arm in the attack. The Coast Guard told me there was a medical missionary here. This was the closest possible help. Our other option was to head on to Ponape."

"Well, let's get onto that help right away," said the American. "Doctor Kitson—that's my wife—is at the clinic at present. We seem to have an epidemic of measles on the island. But I saw your boat approaching, so I came down to greet you. We don't get too many visitors here. By the way, my name is Philip Kitson." He held out his right hand and Barker shook it, saying, "Oh, er, wonderful. I'm James Barker. We are from Canada."

"Your boat will be completely safe here," said Kitson. "Is Andrea able to walk up to the clinic? It's not too far."

"I'll fetch her, and we'll come right away," replied Barker. He went on board his boat and appeared a few minutes later helping Andrea onto the dock. He had also pulled on a shirt. "Andrea," he said to Kitson, then to her, "Honey, this is Philip Kitson. His wife is a doctor, and we are going to the clinic which is close by."

Philip Kitson was full of sympathy as he noted Andrea's white face and the obvious pain she was in. "Dorothy will take care of this in no time," he said to her kindly, and led the way to the steps and footpath which led to the clinic. On the way they passed a neat little white cottage surrounded by flowerbeds in a riot of colour. "Our place," Philip said, with a brief wave of one arm. The locals live in much simpler dwellings, all over the place. These are just a few." And again he pointed with a sweeping motion to several simple structures made from poles and woven palm leaves.

They reached the clinic and found that it was a rectangular building which matched the Kitson's cottage in construction and colour. Entering, they found Dorothy Kitson busy at a small desk. She jumped up as they approached.

"Dorothy, this is James Barker and Andrea....They sailed in a few minutes ago, and Andrea has broken her arm." As her husband finished speaking, Dorothy Kitson took Andrea's right arm and led her to a high bed which served as her 'operating' table.

"Just lie down here, dear," she said gently. "Let me take a look. Philip, why don't you take Mister Barker to the cottage. There's no sense in hanging around the measles."

Leaving Andrea in capable hands, Barker walked with Philip Kitson to the cottage. On the way, Kitson remarked, "James, you must be pretty upset about the damage to your yacht. I want you to tell me about the shark attack. But first," he paused and glanced at Barker, "I'm sure you would like to clean up a little while I fix us something to drink. How about some lemonade?"

Barker thanked him and was shown to the bathroom. Looking in the mirror, he noticed for the first time his unshaven appearance and unkempt dark wavy hair. He looked all the more uncouth by the dried blood which had congealed down the side of his head and face.

He cleaned up as best as he could, but the cut had begun to bleed again, so he held a wad of toilet paper to the side of his head.

When he returned to the little living room where two glasses of lemonade were waiting, Kitson exclaimed, "James! Let me get you something to put on the cut."

"No, don't worry about it," said Barker hurriedly, "The cut itself is on the side of my head, in my hair. It will stop bleeding in a minute." He removed the wad of tissue and sure enough, the blood had ceased flowing.

Sitting with a magnificent view of the big lagoon inside the reef, and the open sea stretching away to the horizon, Barker was quiet for a moment. Then he turned to Kitson and related the events leading up to their meeting on the dock. Philip Kitson was plainly interested and listened intently. He remarked that he had not heard of such an attack before, but that the local fishermen had occasionally encountered huge sharks. Such encounters were always life-threatening affairs, and were reported to the folk on shore in such a manner as to produce great fear.

"What about your boat?" asked Kitson. "Can you repair it here before you set off again?"

"Well, I will have to do some kind of repair work. It would not be safe to sail off without a backstay, and I don't fancy having that gaping hole in the stern. If we encountered big following seas, we would take on a lot of water."

"Do you carry the right kind of materials with you?"

"Yes, I do have a fair amount of repair kit, the fibreglass cloth and resin and so forth. But, the stern guard-railing replacement is a job for a professional. That will have to wait until we get to Australia."

The two men heard the cottage door opening and closing again, and Dorothy entered with her arm protectively around Andrea's shoulder. Barker could see the plaster cast on her other arm and he went forward to take her hand.

"How are you feeling, honey?" he asked, and she nodded and

gave him a weak little smile.

Dorothy Kitson spoke up then. "Andrea's arm was badly broken. There were multiple breaks to some of the bones, probably caused when her body weight pressed the arm against the metal railing, as she has explained to me. But, I have done the best that I can do with my facilities, and I have administered all the other necessary drugs. Now," she continued, "it would be best if Andrea slept here in the cottage. She will need further pain killers and must keep the arm as still and free from any jarring, as possible."

There was a pause and then Dorothy spoke again. "It would be helpful, James, and I'm sure Andrea would appreciate it too, if you spent the night here as well. There are two beds in our little spare room. Would that be acceptable?"

"That is very kind of you!" exclaimed Barker. "We did not expect to put you to so much trouble. I will go to the boat and collect some clothes and things. *Hon,* do you need anything in particular?"

"Just my pyjamas and toiletries," Andrea replied. "Oh, and please bring our little 'brag-book.'"

Barker left the cottage and hurried to his boat. Once on board, he quickly shaved using his battery powered razor and followed up by running a comb through his hair. Then he gathered up some clothes and toiletries and put these, together with their little photo album, in a duffle bag. He locked all the hatches and checked the lines and fenders securing the Robson to the dock. Satisfied, he returned to the cottage and found that Philip Kitson had prepared an early tasty looking supper of sliced ham and a freshly picked garden salad for the four of them.

3

While the Kitsons tidied up the kitchen after eating, James helped Andrea undress and slip on the long tee-shirt — as pyjamas. She was feeling pretty exhausted after her ordeal, and Dorothy Kitson had given her two sedative tablets, suggesting she get an early night. Barker pulled back the light blanket and clean white sheets and helped Andrea into one of the beds in the spare room they had been shown. Then, he tucked her in and kissed her on the forehead.

"Can I get you anything else?" he asked her, softly.

"No," she whispered. "Honey, what are we going to do?"

"We are going to stay here for a while. I will make some repairs—the ones I can do—and I will find out where we need to take *Skipping Stone* for repairs that a shop needs to make. While your arm heals, we can catch up on the letters we need to write to family and friends."

She nodded, and her eyes closed sleepily. Barker gave her another light kiss and whispered, "I am going to join them and be sociable for a while. They are being very kind to us. You have a good sleep, and I will be coming back to you pretty soon. Love you."

He went through to the living room and both Philip and Dorothy looked up at him as he entered. For the first time, Dorothy really noticed how slim, tall, and tanned Barker was, and she liked his square-cut facial features and how the strikingly blue eyes gazed steadily at her husband and herself. Philip pointed to the tea tray and said, "Help yourself, James."

Barker poured his tea and sat in an easy chair facing the Kitsons on the love-seat. There was a short silence and then Dorothy spoke.

"James, Philip told me you are from Canada. Have you and Andrea sailed from there?"

Barker sipped his tea before replying. "Yes. It's quite a long story. Andrea and I met at university in Victoria. She was studying to be a teacher, and I was doing post-graduate work in the Astronomy Department. We both wanted to travel before settling down, and I have always had this dream of sailing around the world."

"Oh," said Philip, "So you had your yacht when you were at university?"

"Yes. Actually I lived on my boat when I was an undergrad student in Vancouver. Before that, I had worked for three years for a company who produced maps of all kinds and descriptions. I was living with my folks in Victoria when I was working, and that enabled me to save every penny, and buy the Robson." Barker glanced at them before he continued, "Victoria is on Vancouver Island. It is the capital of British Columbia, and I returned there to finish my post-grad work."

"Interesting," remarked Philip Kitson. "You have obviously done lots of sailing and are very comfortable living on board a yacht. I have often wondered what that would be like…and also, the other thing you mentioned, maps. I have wondered, too, how maps are made. You call your boat 'the Robson.' Is that its name? Anyway, I'm sorry for all these questions. Please carry on."

Barker drank more of his tea. "No problem. The yacht is a Robson Thirty-two, that's the make and model of the boat. Its name is *Skipping Stone*. Oh yes, where was I? Maps. Yes, that was interesting work. The division I worked in produced maps from aerial photographs. It was pretty straight forward stuff, no magic to it. But, in other methods of map making, fairly complicated geometrical extrapolations and mathematics is involved. Anyway, back to sailing. My dad and mom loved sailing, and the waters around Victoria are just perfect for that. There are so many islands and marine parks to explore, and lots of sheltered coves and little harbours to duck into when the weather gets unkind. They took my sister and me on their sailboat—a thirty five foot ketch—almost from the day we were born. So, I grew up to love sailing."

Dorothy Kitson spoke up, "James, I'm afraid I know very little about sailing. But I do have two questions for you. Firstly, *Skipping Stone* sounds unusual as a name. What does it mean? And secondly, what is a ketch?"

"Sorry," Barker replied, "Yes, I named my boat *Skipping Stone* after those flat stones we used to throw out and try to bounce on the water when we were kids. I liked the idea of my boat, under full sail, even though she is quite heavy, skipping along through the waves, hence the name. And a ketch is a sailboat with two masts, and the tall one is in the front. You've heard of a schooner?" he paused and glanced at them, and they both nodded. "Well, a schooner has more than one mast, too. But a schooner's tall mast is at the back, behind the shorter mast. Now, my boat *Skipping Stone*, is a sloop, a Marconi-rigged sloop, to be precise. That means she has one mast and the mainsail is triangle-shaped and hauled up the mast by the halyard which is connected to the top of the triangle, or sharp point of the sail. It also means she has only one sail in front of the mast, not two, like a cutter. Oh, boy! Sailboats have so many working parts, and so many strange sounding names for those parts. It can seem pretty confusing in the beginning."

"My my!" exclaimed Dorothy. "There is so much more to this than I ever imagined. James, the only sailing we have ever done, is on the funny little boats these islanders have. They take us across to neighbouring islands when there is a medical emergency there, or when Philip goes to teach."

Barker looked up. "So you are a teacher, Philip?"

"Sort of," replied Kitson, "But tell us, how long has it taken you to get here? I mean, from Canada?"

Barker looked at Dorothy again. "Those funny little boats the locals sail in, have two hulls, right?" She nodded, and said, "Yes, like two canoes, sort of strapped together with poles. Catamarans, I believe they are called."

Barker nodded. "Yes, and they cross oceans in those! Well, to answer your question, Philip: Andrea and I left Vancouver five months ago. We sailed down the west coast, down past Washington, Oregon and about half-way down the California coast. Then we turned out into the Pacific to catch the trade winds to Hawaii. If you try to sail to Hawaii straight from Canada, that is, from Vancouver Island, you're into headwinds the whole way. So, it's best to hug the coast until you are in line with the trade winds that blow westward before you head out to sea.

"We had very good conditions on our way to Hawaii, and I was so pleased. Andrea had only sailed for one year with me, and in those sheltered waters off Victoria, so she started out a little nervous. But she got into it very quickly and began to love it. In no time at all she was a competent sailor, and I could leave her in control of the Robson and take a lengthy nap.

"It took us thirty nine days to reach Hawaii. That's pretty good going for a small sailboat, and we made landfall on Oahu, and spent three weeks in Honolulu. After stocking up our provisions for a long ocean crossing, we sailed out of the marina near the city and headed west, to pass north of the Marshall Islands. When we had gone a little west of Wake Island, at about one hundred and sixty five degrees east longitude, I set a more southerly course for the Carolines. It took us twenty seven days to reach that point, and we encountered only one bit of bad weather.... Several days of flat calm, though."

"Fascinating stuff!" said Philip. "Did you see any whales or catch any fish as you went along?"

"Let me just check on Andrea for a moment, and I'll be right back," Barker said, and he went through to the spare room.

Returning to his seat again, he continued. "She's fine, sleeping now. Well, life out on the open ocean is all I ever dreamed it would be. Andrea fell in love with it, too. Yes, we saw whales quite often, and once or twice a little too close for comfort. Some ocean-going yachts have collided with whales and sunk at sea. I guess it's the quietness, no engine throbbing away to warn the whales of the boat's presence.

"And yes, I trailed a lure behind the Robson most of the time. We caught fish on many occasions, and once I had something on that was so big I could not pull in the line. Hand line, you see. I don't know what it was, eventually it broke free. But for a while it stopped us dead in our tracks! Of course flying fish came on board regularly, and we ate a lot of fish."

"Whales and collisions!" exclaimed Philip. "I have never thought such a thing might happen. So, it's the silence that's the problem, is it? No engine sound to warn the whales. You know, James, cars can have a special whistle attached to the undercarriage and it sends out a signal to deer and other wildlife on the roads, warning them that a vehicle is approaching. I wonder if such a device could work to warn whales of an approaching sailboat?"

"That's an interesting thought," said Barker. "Maybe you should experiment along those lines, Philip. You make the whistle, and I will try it out for you?"

Kitson smiled. "When did you first notice the shark, James?"

"It was when we were only about fifty miles out, I would say," replied Barker. "Yes, about fifty miles out from here, that's when we first noticed the Great White. It followed us for many hours, a huge monster. Andrea guessed it was about twenty five feet in length. Then, early this morning it attacked. By the time I had Andrea inside on the settee, and had found my pistol, it had decided to leave."

"You carry a gun with you?" asked Dorothy.

"Yes, just a small side arm, an automatic pistol. I carry it for emergencies like the one we went through with the shark, and also to discourage pirates and protect ourselves in some of the strange places we visit on shore."

"Did you take photographs of some of the highlights on the way?" asked Dorothy. "Andrea mentioned her brag—book, a small album, I gather. Are your wedding pictures in there?"

"We have taken many photos along the way, and we use a digital camera, now," said Barker, "and it stores up to one hundred and twenty pictures on the memory chip. I also have a laptop computer on the Robson and I download the pictures onto the computer once the chip gets close to filling up. That way I can edit and delete poor shots and also clear the camera chip to make room for more photos."

"We would love to see them, if that's possible," said Philip.

"Sure, that's no problem, I'd love to show them to you," said James, before turning to face Dorothy. "And there are no wedding pictures in the brag book, just pictures of our families and friends and stuff. Andrea and I are not married. We just live together."

"Ah...I see," said Philip. "Hmm...tell me, James, you have a post graduate degree in astronomy?"

"Yes," Barker replied, "I graduated with a Masters shortly before we left."

"If you don't mind me asking," said Philip, "what sort of job prospects are there these days for an astronomer? What work might you be doing, and where might you end up?"

"Well," said Barker, "with the space program in full swing now, there are some jobs available not only in the US, but in Canada and several other countries which are cooperating together in various space exploration or service development research programs. And, of course, there are always teaching jobs opening up for astronomers, so I will just keep looking at the whole field once we get home."

"And where is home likely to be, James? Do you have a preference for the place you would like to live?"

Barker stretched and then replied, "Philip, if I had an open choice, I would go for Vancouver Island as the place to live. But, although there are teaching possibilities there, and an observatory, too, the place is number one choice for Canadians to live. That makes getting a job there, difficult. Most likely, I will end up either in the States, working for NASA, or in Australia with a cooperative program with NASA."

"Would you like that? I mean, living in Australia?" asked Dorothy.

"Yeah," replied James. "I guess there is always some excitement around living in another country for a while, at least. Andrea and I would like to travel a bit before we have kids, so a job in Ozzy would be pretty good, I reckon."

"What about your folks back home, in Canada," asked Dorothy, "and Andrea's family? Are they happy for you to be so far away?"

"Sure," replied Barker. "We are making our own way in life now, so..."

It was quiet in the room for a while and Barker noticed that the Kitsons were looking at the floor. Then Philip spoke quietly, "James, you've had a tough day. Take a bath or a shower, whichever you prefer, and turn in. We are tired, too. Now, tomorrow, join us for breakfast at about eight, and we'll take things from there. Okay?"

Barker nodded, and yawned. "Thanks for all your kindness," he said. "Thank you Dorothy. Please let me know what I owe you for the medical treatment you gave Andrea. And thanks for your hospitality, for having us stay here in your cottage."

"You are most welcome," they both said in unison, and Dorothy continued, "James, we very seldom have visitors here to Big Truk, at least, not visitors from North America! So, feel free to stay as long as you like. Andrea will need to be careful with that arm, and you can stay and make the repairs necessary on *Skipping Stone*. Please, don't hurry off!"

Barker smiled and said, "You are both very kind." Then he left for the spare bedroom.

4

On a lovely beach some twenty miles west of Big Truk Island, Jimmy Bartholomew, the Second Mate on the US Coast Guard ship USCG401, was restless. Sitting up so suddenly that he startled his wife Amy, he exclaimed, "I'm bored!"

Amy rolled over and adjusted the bust line of her swimsuit. "What's up with you Jimmy?" she asked, teasingly, "here we are in heaven, and you are bored?"

"No, babe," he replied, "I'm not bored with *you,* it's my job. You don't understand. I know that I pushed for this assignment here in the Carolines, but it's been four years now. And the routine is killing me. Every day it's the same. Up at six a.m.; breakfast at six-thirty; clean-up duties 'til nine. Can you understand that? The blessed ship is already as clean as a whistle that's been polished between a Bedouin's backside and a camel's hump, and Yuruchuk says, 'Clean her, boys!'"

Amy grinned. "The captain is a good guy, Jimmy, you told me so yourself. You said that he's the finest kind you've ever served under, remember?"

"Yeah," groaned Bartholomew, "I know. He's a good guy, but after clean-up, then what? He says to us a while back, 'Okay fellas, you are starting to show some signs of *easy livin*. I see fat-rolls that would shame a prize manatee-cross-blubber seal on some of you. I think it's time for some exercises!' For the past four months, now, we have run, climbed the gym bars, pressed weights, swum hundreds of yards each morning, and rowed the life-boats for miles. Anyone would think he's trying to coach a team for the Iron Man Olympics, or somethin!"

Amy chuckled and leaned forward and planted a soft kiss on Jimmy's lips.

"Hey, babe," he gasped, "that's not good for my blood pressure!"

"Come, honey, let's go for a swim then, and you can cool off" said Amy, with a sly look, and she stood to her feet.

"No, sweetie," said Jimmy, "You go in, I'm through with swimming for a day or two."

He sat and watched as Amy walked down to the water's edge, admiring her figure. Then his thoughts turned to the news report that he had heard that morning when he and Amy had been breakfasting on the pancakes he had made and the maple syrup she had brought over with her. Being on leave here was delightful, he admitted to himself, and in general, life was very good. Having Amy visiting from Stateside was like the cherry on the top and he knew he had nothing to really complain about. But, there was that news report. What did the guy say? *Something about an unusual number of sightings of Great White Sharks, and some brutal encounters with them during the past two months. Two bathers killed, five fishing-or pleasure-boats attacked, and some strange things observed by those marine biologist guys.*

Amy had reached the water and felt it gingerly with her toes. It was warm and inviting. She looked out over the turquoise sea in the little bay before her and then looked back at the way her feet had sunk down in the wet golden sand. As she did so, something registered in her mind as though she had just caught a fleeting glimpse of a dark object about twenty yards out. Startled, she looked up quickly and was just in time to see what looked like a huge shadow disappearing into the depths. A feeling of fear came over her and she retreated away from the water's edge. Staring out to the place she had intended to swim to, it all looked peaceful and the perfect picture of a tropical paradise.

Twenty feet below the surface of the gentle swells which were rolling lazily into the beach, all peace had vanished. The shark's appearance had caused all other marine life to flee to safety or take refuge in their burrows and tunnels on the sea bed. The great beast was hungry. It was also feeling the painful consequences of its previous and unsuccessful attack on the strange creature it had encountered near Truk Island. Several of its teeth had been broken in that incident although these would be replaced by the marvellous built-in mechanism in which new rows of teeth constantly move forward to replace old ones. So it continued to swim in a wide circle in front of the beach where more than a dozen holiday makers were sunbathing.

Oh well, thought Amy, *I'm imagining things, there can't be a submarine this close to shore ... I'll just have a quick dip to cool off.*

About to move down to the sea's edge again, she felt a sharp pain in her right foot and yelped. It was a thorn, and she bent down and pulled it from her instep. Bartholomew had heard his wife's yelp and he looked up to see what was wrong. At that moment, and only thirty yards away behind Amy, a huge fin slid down into the water and disappeared from sight. He gaped in astonishment, wondering if his thoughts about the news report had caused an image to materialise in front of his eyes. Jumping to his feet, he hurried over to Amy's side and reached her just as she straightened up. Showing him the thorn which she held in her hand, he instantly realised what had caused her to yelp in pain. However, it was that other thing that filled his mind.

"Amy, I just saw something out there," he said pointing behind her towards the sea.

"That's *funny,*" she said slowly, "I thought I did, too. In fact I thought I was seeing things. I couldn't believe my eyes. That's why I backed off from going into the water just a minute ago."

"What did you see?" Jimmy asked.

"I don't really know," she said, frowning. "But, it was darkish, not actually black or anything, but huge like a small submarine. Surely a sub couldn't come in this close could it?"

"No, but a really big shark could!" he said grimly. "And I was sitting there and remembering the news report I saw, *that we saw,* this morning. Do you recall it?"

She shook her head.

"Yes," continued Bartholomew, "I heard them saying that there have been an unusual number of sightings and even attacks by Great White sharks recently. I wonder if that's what we caught a glimpse of?"

"Well, one thing is for sure," said Amy, shivering, "I'm not going in the water again! Come, let's go up to our room at the resort."

Jimmy Bartholomew took her hand and said, "First I must warn the other folk on the beach. We don't want someone eaten by a Great White while we are here!"

With that he led his wife over to where other sun-worshippers were lying on the sand. When he came up to them, he let Amy's hand go and whistled shrilly. Most of the people looked up at him.

"Folks," he shouted loudly, "please give me your attention. My wife and I have both just seen what might be a dangerous shark quite close inshore, right here, on this beach. My advice is to keep out of the water for a while."

Amy stood watching him admiringly. She knew her Jimmy was a United States Navy Officer, but she had never seen him displaying his leadership and authority before. The holiday makers quickly gathered around them and started firing questions. Bartholomew simply held up his hands and they grew quiet.

"I'm simply giving you some advice," he said, quietly. "I would not want to see nor hear that one of you was maimed or killed by a man eater. The shark we *both* saw," and he emphasised the 'both' in his sentence, "was only about twenty or twenty-five yards out from the water's edge. Just this morning I heard a news report about unusual sightings of Great White sharks, and even several attacks on boats and bathers. So, *we* are not going in again until the coast is clear once more!" Then, taking Amy's hand, together they made their way back to the beachfront hotel where they were vacationing, leaving a buzz of conversation behind them.

5

James Barker awoke shortly after six the next morning. Andrea was still soundly asleep, so he dressed quietly and left the cottage. Approaching *Skipping Stone* he again examined the damage the shark had inflicted on his yacht. It was astonishing. He marvelled at the sheer brute force of the monster fish and thought that Andrea and he had been very lucky to have got off so lightly.

The damage to the hull of the Robson was high up on the counter stern, and Barker felt confident he could repair it. He knew he would not feel safe continuing on the journey without closing up the jagged hole. He could easily picture the waves in a following sea breaking against the stern when the boat was running down wind. If the hole was there, the boat could take on a lot of water, maybe even enough to cause serious problems....

Climbing on board, he looked at the business end of the backstay, with its deck mounting still attached. Even that problem, Barker believed he could remedy. It would take plenty of fibreglass reinforcing, but would not be too difficult to fix at the same time that he repaired the stern.

Unlocking the cabin, he went below and found his wallet and the wad of US dollars he kept for visits ashore. Removing two hundred, he carefully stowed the remaining notes in the cunningly concealed lock-box on the side of the chain locker for his anchor. Then, he secured everything again, and returned to the cottage.

Upon entering and on his way to check whether Andrea was awake, he noticed that both Kitsons were sitting quietly in the living room. They were both reading, and neither looked up as he passed by. Andrea was awake, so he knelt at the side of her bed and took her right hand gently in his. "How are you feeling, hon?" he asked her softly.

She nodded. "I had a good sleep, and my arm is not so painful this morning. Oh, it was *so sore* last night. I thought I would never be able to sleep."

"Oh dear," said Barker, "but it's good that you did finally get some sleep. Philip and Dorothy are both awake. They were in the living room, reading, but they didn't seem to notice me when I came in. Look, let's go and take a bath. That's a luxury we haven't been able to take for weeks."

When they emerged from the spare room on their way to the bathroom, the Kitsons were no longer in the living room. James ran the hot and cold water into the tub, and then he helped Andrea slip out of her night dress. He shaved while she climbed into the bath and soaked for a while, the warm, fresh water feeling very good. She held her left arm, in its plaster cast, on the side of the tub, to keep it dry, and managed quite well to wash with one hand. Drying herself turned out to be very difficult, and Barker came to the rescue. Then, while she dressed, he scrubbed himself in the tub and after drying himself with the towel provided by Dorothy, he dressed and was ready to join the others at the breakfast table.

After the morning greetings, Dorothy enquired how Andrea had slept, and how her arm was feeling. Then, they all tucked in to hot oatmeal porridge, sweetened with condensed milk, before finishing with delicious island-grown mangos. Moving out into the warm sunshine, Philip led the way to where he had placed four folding chairs facing the sea. Dorothy joined them carrying a tray with mugs and freshly brewed tea.

They sat quietly for a few minutes, savouring the peace of the morning. Then, Philip broke the silence. "Dorothy has her normal work to attend to at the clinic this morning, and I need to prepare for a teaching I am due to give on the other side of the island tomorrow. Dorothy and I would dearly love for you two to stay on for as long as you can. It is so nice for us to have company."

"Yes, dear," said Dorothy, and she put her hand on Andrea's arm. "Please stay on with us. You two can make yourselves at home in the cottage, help yourselves to tea and whatever snacks you can find, and just relax, keeping that arm as still as possible for a few days. Then, if you would like, you could join us when we go across to Little Truk for the day next Monday."

James and Andrea accepted the invitation readily, and finishing their tea, they remained outside while both Philip and Dorothy went off to their respective duties. Andrea began to doze, surprised at how sleepy she felt even after such a good night's rest. Barker noticed this, and stood up. Leaning over, he whispered in her ear. "I'm going to make a start on the repairs, honey. Just relax here, and I will come back in a short while."

6

Several miles inside the reef surrounding Truk Island, the two dark-skinned islanders were preparing their lines for the day's fishing. Shortly before sunrise, they had left the lagoon where Barker's boat was docked. Three other sailing catamarans had accompanied Pikelot and his friend Farulap, and all four craft had headed for the same spot, about halfway to Hall Island. There was an underwater reef at that place, and it teemed with rockfish, parrot-fish, trigger-fish, and many different species all of which were good eating.

Now, as the sun became very warm, the boats were dispersed over an area about one acre in extent. Lines were prepared, hooks were baited, and these were lowered to the ocean floor below. As each fisherman felt the bait touch the reef, he quickly raised it several feet to minimise snagging on the sharp edges of volcanic rock in the depths below his boat.

Pikelot and Farulap each sat in one of the canoe-like hulls of the catamaran with their own lines and bait and spare tackle. They were separated from each other by the platform of slim branches woven together and tied to the stout poles which were lashed to each hull. On this platform lay the lateen sail they had lowered after arriving at the favoured fishing spot.

It was turning out to be a productive day. Farulap had

accumulated fifteen plump fish of various kinds in the hull, and he heard them flapping behind him from time to time. Pikelot was having similar luck. Then, suddenly, the fish went off the bite. This was unusual, and Pikelot turned to face his friend. "Hey, Farulap! Have you excreted in the water? What have you done to so frighten the fish, my ugly partner?" he said affectionately.

Greetings and comments like these were common among these islanders, and westerners were often shocked by them when they learned the local language. But to the islanders, and even on the larger land-masses such as New Guinea, the more 'disgusting' a greeting was, the more affectionate was the intention.

Farulap grunted and was about to reply with a much more colourful 'compliment' when his world was shattered by something that to a westerner would have resembled a Polaris missile bursting forth from the depths of the sea.

The Great White shark that had attacked *Skipping Stone* the previous day, had swum away in frustration after breaking several rows of its teeth on the hard fibreglass hull of the yacht. The creature it had clearly seen moving about on the *thing which swam along the surface*, had not fallen into the sea. This had disappointed the shark and it had attacked several more times, and much more aggressively. Then, it had dived feeling a mild and irritating pain in its mouth.

Carcharodon carcharias is a mackerel shark which starts out bluish in colour when young but becomes very large and almost white when it reaches maturity. Commonly reaching lengths of twenty feet or more, and frequently found in warm seas, the Great White shark, or simply, Great White, strikes terror in the hearts of bathers and surfers alike. The specimen which had inflicted such damage to James Barker's boat, had prowled about in search of prey and had only managed to gulp down a hapless grouper that it cornered on one of the reefs in the area. Then it had swum west along the archipelago and had cruised along the beaches of several islands, but without success in finding a meal. Returning to the vicinity of the Truk clusters of islands, it had dived to the reefs below. Ravenously hungry despite the fact that a seventy pound grouper had not satisfied its rapacious appetite, it continued its search for prey. It was then that it had become aware of the fleet of small craft on the surface. Remembering that the strategy it had employed the day before had not been successful, the huge fish decided not to surface this time to check out these floating objects. Instead, in its primitive brain, it made the decision to surprise whatever prey might be relaxing above by leaping from the depths and literally falling upon them.

Aiming at a spot about ten feet from one of these floating objects, the monster fish propelled itself upwards at high speed. Reaching the surface, it almost completely cleared the water before crashing down onto the platform structure between the two startled fishermen. The devastating impact of the colossal shark caused the relatively frail catamaran to fold in two, projecting both men into the air as though bounced from a trampoline.

Tragically for Pikelot, he descended directly in front of the beast's nose and with a reflex action, those terrible jaws seized him and separated his upper torso from his legs. Farulap had an impression of blood spraying out like a curtain and turning all he could see crimson. Then he fell back into the half submerged hull that his friend had occupied moments before, cracking his head on the catamaran's hard side. He lost consciousness, and was unaware of the events that followed.

All six occupants in the remainder of the fishing fleet witnessed the death of Pikelot, but only two of the men saw the beginning of the drama when the Great White leaped from the water. In panic they all cast away their fishing lines and began paddling in a frantic effort to escape from the vicinity of the shark. In the next few minutes, a similar fate had engulfed two of the other catamarans and their occupants. In these cases, the shark killed all four fishermen, even devouring one of the terrified men as he tried to swim away.

Then, as suddenly as it had begun, it ended. All became still and silence descended on the ocean above the reef. The one surviving catamaran was speeding away from the scene as fast as the two fishermen inside could paddle it. After about ten minutes, they raised their sail and headed for home, neither speaking a single word.

Back near the place which had so recently been a center of carnage, Farulap lay stunned in the remaining wreckage of Pikelot's catamaran. Gradually the cool water which half filled the hull in which he lay, began to revive him. He stirred and opened his eyes. Immediately he became aware of the pain which throbbed in his head and he groaned. Slowly, he sat up and the sight of the wreck all around him brought back the vivid memory of those terrifying moments when his world had shattered. He looked around, and noticed the wreckage of two of the other craft, and that their occupants had disappeared. There was no sign of the third catamaran.

Farulap slumped in his position, put his head in his hands, and great wracking sobs shook his frame. After a minute or two, he sat up straight again. He gathered his wits and began removing the remnants of the broken platform from his canoe-like portion of the catamaran. Glancing around, he spotted a paddle floating near by, and he used his hands to move his canoe nearer to retrieve it.

Then, very fearfully, and very carefully, he paddled towards Truk Island.

7

Back on his yacht in the peaceful lagoon James Barker made a start on the repairs to his boat by selecting the tools he thought he might need. These tools were kept in clear strong plastic bags to minimise corrosion while at sea. Carrying his selection to the cockpit, Barker used his hacksaw to cut away some of the jagged ends of the broken guard rails. This was a tedious job and kept him busy until the heat of the sun drove him back to the cottage. He was alarmed to find Andrea asleep and severely sun-burned. He quickly awakened her and led her inside. But the damage was done, and she began to feel nauseous and quickly developed a severe headache.

Barker was astonished by this. Andrea had seemed to him to have gained a deep tan during their voyage. He was wondering how this day's relatively brief session in the sun could have caused such a reaction, when he realized that she had lain for four hours in the burning rays. Always before, she had been very careful to apply a thick coating of sunscreen to her bare skin, and had often retreated from the fierce midday sun's rays by reading in *Skipping Stone's* saloon. However, on this occasion, Andrea had fallen asleep, still under the effects of some of the drugs she had received.

Barker gave her a large glass of cool water from the refrigerator, and insisted that she drink it while he waited. Then, he searched in the bathroom closet and found some aspirin. Andrea swallowed the recommended dose with more water. Then he led her to the spare room and helped her onto the bed. He pulled the drapes at the window and darkened the room. "Andy," he said to her, "I'm going to find Dorothy. I want her to see you when she gets a break at the clinic."

Leaving the cottage, Barker hurried up to the clinic and found both Philip and Dorothy beginning to walk back to the cottage for their lunch break. He informed them of Andrea's condition, and they all quickened their pace. When they arrived, they were relieved to find that her headache had eased and she had not vomited up all the liquids. Barker felt quite embarrassed over the whole affair, and not a little guilty that he had spent such a long period away working on his boat. Andrea did not feel like eating, so he joined the Kitsons at the lunch table and enjoyed the sandwiches Philip had made.

Since Dorothy was remaining at the cottage that afternoon, and said she would keep an eye on Andrea, Barker stood up to excuse himself and return to his repairs. However he felt a restraining hand from Philip on his arm, and he paused.

"I would like to come with you," Philip said. "However, it is not wise to work outside during these midday hours of intense heat. Look, it is only two fifteen in the afternoon. Why don't you and I sit in the shade on the side of the house, and shoot the breeze until it cools down a little?"

Appreciating the wisdom in Philip's suggestion, Barker agreed and followed Kitson outside. Each picking up a chair, they moved into the shade and sat down. It was Barker who decided that he would get in first with questions.

"Philip," he began, "tell me about yourself. I understood from the US Coast Guard in Ponape that you are here on some sort of missionary assignment. Where are you from? And what led you and

Dorothy to this isolated place?"

Philip smiled, looking at him. "James," he said, "I trained as an accountant and was employed by a large firm in the States for twenty four years. I met Dorothy two years after I started work. She was an intern at the hospital in our city, and we married and soon two children had arrived. I was a *work-a-holic*, and neglected both her and our children. Soon I was earning a six-figure salary, and bringing home a huge bonus every year.

"Dorothy tried to juggle her time between the children's growing needs, and her own need to keep her hand in as a medical doctor. Something had to give. Our son ran away from home and was tragically killed in an automobile accident when he was twelve. On the same day that we got the news, our daughter, aged fifteen, told us she was pregnant. Kitson paused for a long moment, and Barker thought that he was still affected by the tragedies. He leaned forward and touched the older man's arm. "Its okay," he said, huskily, "I did not mean for you to suffer through these memories."

To the younger man's surprise, Kitson looked up and smiled peacefully. "James," he said, "Of course it was tough, *desperately sad*. But we've come through it all now, both Dorothy and I. Let me continue. I told you our daughter, our oldest child, had fallen pregnant when she was fifteen. She had the child and we made her put it out for adoption. It broke her heart, and she turned to drugs.

"There I was, a very wealthy man. A top executive, and highly respected in my field. I had been invited onto the board of directors of several large corporations. I was invited to speak at special gatherings and to meetings of young executives and final year students in many business schools. Everyone thought I was Mister Success.

"But I knew, down on the inside, that I was Mister Failure. I had failed as a husband, and I had failed dreadfully as a father. The only reason that Dorothy stayed with me was because I left her alone and she could do whatever she pleased.

He paused and gazed out to sea for several minutes, before speaking again. "Then one day—it was a Saturday—I went for a walk along the beach where we had our waterfront home. I had gone about a mile or so, and I sat down on a log which was high up on the sand dunes. I began to think about my life again and the terrible mess and tragedies in all of it. I knew that although it was too late for parts of it to be turned around, nevertheless I longed with all my heart for some miracle to change me. So deep was the agony in my heart that I cried out to God for help. I remember saying, *'God, if You are up there, please help me, show me what I must do to turn things around.'*

Kitson paused again before continuing. "As I sat there waiting, a scripture verse that I must have heard as a child when attending Sunday school, came to mind. It says: *What does it profit a man that he should gain the entire world, yet lose his soul?* I realised then, that all of my worldly success meant nothing in the final analysis. What was most important was my relationship with my wife and children. I broke down and sobbed. Then, a great sense of peace suddenly settled upon me. Now, I am not a religious man. I am not one who goes to church meetings. But I want to tell you that *I know* that God spoke to my heart that Saturday. I heard Him say in my mind, that if I followed through with my intentions to repent, then He would bring a restoration into my life that would make me *marvel!*"

At this point, Barker stood up and flexed his shoulders, staring out to sea. Then he turned to Philip and spoke, "What makes you so sure it was God who spoke to you? Isn't it possible that your own resolve to change your ways brought about improvements in your life?"

Philip smiled. "Of course it is possible," he said. "But the strange thing about it was that I had made those same resolutions for the previous seven years! I had even told Dorothy I was going to quit my job, and that we would move to a quiet place, etcetera. I had done that many times! *But I had never had the guts to follow through.* But, when I heard that voice in my mind, something happened inside me. I walked into the office the following Monday morning and handed in my resignation. Then I went home and phoned Dorothy at the clinic where she did stand-in work. I asked her out to dinner, and she almost fainted." He chuckled as he remembered. Then there was along pause again, before he spoke.

"I took her to a quiet little restaurant and I told her what had happened and what I had done. She was stunned, and was quiet for a long while. But I waited for her response."

"What did she do?" asked Barker.

"She stood up from the table and said something I was totally unprepared for. In fact, what she said boggled my mind." Philip went silent and looked out to sea.

8

On the lawn in the shade of the house, Philip Kitson was about to resume his conversation with Barker when shouts were heard from the vicinity of the lagoon. The two men stood to their feet and looked down to the dock to see what the commotion was about. A catamaran was in the lagoon and the two men on board were shouting at the top of their voices. Within minutes, Islanders began appearing on the beach and a great wailing began to fill the air.

Kitson turned to Barker and said, "Something tragic has happened. Do you hear that wailing? These Islanders wail like that when someone dies. I had better go down there and find out more."

They hurried down to the dock and turned at the foot of the steps to go onto the beach. The catamaran had come ashore and about twenty locals were gathered around the two fishermen who were describing the catastrophe that had happened out at the reef. Philip, who had learned the language, related their story to Barker. The wives and families of the fishermen who were killed by the shark, were almost besides themselves with grief.

James Barker left Kitson commiserating with the bereaved families, and wandered away from the crowd. He went onto the dock and walked toward his boat, deep in thought. *The Great White had struck again.* These Islanders survived on the fish they caught. It was a major source of protein in their diet, and if fear of that killer shark spread among the fishermen, the welfare of the whole community would be threatened. Something *had* to be done to help them.

Barker heard footsteps on the dock behind him and turned to see Kitson approaching. "Six men were killed out there," he said. This is a crisis for these people, and fear could very well prevent them from fishing."

"Yes, Philip," said Barker quietly, as the older man looked closely at him. "And fish is almost their only source of protein. If they try to live on fruit and root crops…" he shook his head. "I was thinking about this just before you got here. We've got to do something!"

Philip Kitson nodded in agreement. He was pleased with the response Barker was showing. Until this point, he had perceived the young man to be self centred and self assured, yet capable of showing great tenderness toward Andrea. There was no doubt in Kitson's mind that Barker was very intelligent, and very resourceful. Now he was observing a degree of compassion in the yachtsman which pleased the older man. As they turned and started to make their way back along the dock to the steps leading up to the cottage, they noticed that the crowd on the beach had gone. The sun was setting and the onset of night was fast approaching. At the foot of the steps, Barker turned to take one last look at his boat and saw something moving across the lagoon. He stopped and looked more carefully.

Kitson saw him and followed the line of his gaze. Then he saw it too. It was a man crouching down and paddling an unusual canoe. The two men moved quickly down the dock as the canoeist brought his craft alongside. Then Philip recognized Farulap, one of the fishermen reported to have been killed by the shark. He helped the man onto the dock and saw the large swelling on the side of his head, and his blood-matted hair.

"Farulap!" Kitson exclaimed. "You are alive! We all thought you were dead, eaten by the big shark. Are the others alive?"

"No, *Wise-one*, they are all dead," said Farulap in a sombre voice.

"What happened to you?" asked Kitson, who once again was interpreting for Barker.

"Pikelot and I were having a good time at the reef. We had both caught plenty of fish, when suddenly they stopped taking our bait. We were wondering what happened, what had caused this problem, when the monster jumped out of the water and swallowed Pikelot." Farulap shuddered at the vivid memory, then continued, becoming more animated, and his voice was stronger.

"The Sky-god you have told us about Wise-one, I believe that He saved me just like you told us He could do. Your God threw me into the sky, out of the reach of the monster, and then placed me in Pikelot's canoe!"

Barker saw Philip reach out and take Farulap's hand and speak to him once more in the Islander's language. Then he saw both men bow their heads and pray. He did not know what they were saying, but it was unmistakably prayer. He stood there awkwardly, wondering whether he should leave, when they opened their eyes and smiled at him.

Kitson then led the way to the cottage, explaining to Barker that he wanted Dorothy to take a look at Farulap's head wound. When this was done, and Farulap hurried off to share the good news of his survival with his family and friends, Philip and Barker found Andrea looking much improved and sitting in the living room. Barker went quickly to her side and sat next to her on the sofa, taking her hand in his. He kissed her on the cheek and asked her how she was feeling. She looked up at him and said softly, "I'm feeling a lot better, honey. The headache's gone, and Dorothy gave me some lotion to ease the sunburn. What happened out there? What was all the wailing about down on the beach?"

Philip related to both women what he had heard from the surviving fishermen, and Andrea shuddered. Turning to Barker, she asked in a querulous voice, "James, do you think that was the same shark that attacked us?"

Barker nodded. "I do," he said. "And I don't think it's a coincidence!"

The others all looked at him, and it was Dorothy who voiced their common thought. "James, what do you mean: 'you don't think it is a coincidence'?"

Barker looked around at the others. "Something's going on here, with us, with Andrea and me, with you folk on this island. I can't put a finger on it, but I have a funny feeling that something *strange* is happening to us."

Silence fell on the group as they all pondered James' words.

Many thousands of miles away from Truk Island, and much further to the north, James Barker's mother Linda, and his sister Ruth, had been praying. The two women met every week in Ruth's apartment in Victoria, British Columbia, to pray for their family members and friends, for the church in Victoria, and for the government.

Linda had spoken to her daughter. "Ruth, dear, these are the things on my heart. First, your father's health; second, James and Andrea. I also want to pray for Gayle Browne, it looks as though her divorce is going through."

Ruth had glanced at her mother, and interjected, "Mom, so Jack is going ahead with it?"

Her mother had nodded, then continued. "Yes, they need much more prayer, those two! And I also want to pray for the government, especially concerning the problems in the Middle East. What's on your heart, dear?"

"It's mostly the same things, really, except I am very burdened for James and Andrea. I don't know why I'm feeling *so burdened,* but I am. The strange thing is, that I am not so concerned about their safety, on the sea, like, you know, but it's something else. And, you know what I mean, Mom!"

"You mean their 'marriage', or rather, them just living together?" Linda Barker had asked.

"Yes, but it's more than that. You know that I spoke to James shortly before they left. I had already chatted to Andrea. She's such a sweet girl. I love her! I *know* she is the one God has chosen for James. You know what, Mom? Andrea was *open!* She listened. I told her what I believed about Christ, and she listened. I could tell she wasn't just being polite, either. What I was saying really seemed to sink in.

"Andrea told me, Mom, that she did believe in God, but didn't know what to do about it! She asked, 'Where do I go from here'? I told her just to pray, to talk with God, and listen for His answers. I told her God's Name is Jesus."

"Oh, that is *wonderful,* Ruth. I didn't know.... but, it's James. He's the problem!"

"No, Mom! James is not the problem. I know that secretly he is searching for answers. But the problem is his head! The university filled his head with garbage. It is all that astronomy stuff he studied. The professors are mostly atheists up there. There are even practicing witches and warlocks on the campus. Anyway, Mom, I want to *really* pray for James, and, Andrea, too. Come on, let's get to it."

As they had been doing regularly for the past six months, the two women had prayed. Linda, prayed sitting, but with her eyes closed; Ruth prayed, walking up and down her living room. Together they had pounded on the gates of Heaven. Sometimes both prayed out loud, simultaneously. At other times, each one spoke while the other was silent, listening. The two prayer-warriors had continued, lifting up their other concerns to their Heavenly Father. They had finished about an hour later, and both felt quite sure that their prayers had not only been heard, but that the answers were on the way…

9

After what happened yesterday, these Islanders need hope and comfort," said Philip Kitson at the breakfast table the next morning.

"Are you going out to meet with them today?" asked Dorothy. "Won't those folk who have lost their loved ones, be in mourning?"

"I believe they need comfort more than anything, right now," replied her husband. "I want to take Farulap with me, too, so that he can share what happened to him. I have a feeling things are coming together!" He looked at his wife and she understood.

"You got any plans, you two?" Dorothy asked, looking from James to Andrea.

"How are you feeling, honey?" James turned to Andrea, who was sitting beside him. "Are you up for a walk, today?"

"Sure," she replied, with a twinkle in her eye. "Where are you going to take me?"

"Philip," said Barker, "I was wondering if Andrea and I could tag along with you today? I know we won't understand any of the language when you do your teaching, but we will see more of the island and perhaps some of the flora and fauna?"

"Oh, that would be *nice!*" Andrea said excitedly, and looked at Philip.

"You are both very welcome to join me," said Philip. "Now, you will need stout walking shoes. There are some bad thorns in the jungle, and I advise you to wear long pants, because of the nettles and spiders that we come into contact with along some of the paths. But, it's not as bad as it sounds. I think that you will enjoy the outing."

The three of them got ready and within thirty minutes they were on their way. Kitson led, with Barker bringing up the rear behind Andrea. Philip had suggested that they not talk for a while, as the silence would increase their chances of seeing wildlife. And indeed it did. They saw several small deer with spotted coats, and once, a wild pig scuttled across their path. However, it was the birds that delighted them most. There was an amazing variety of brightly coloured tropical birds that flitted from tree to tree with loud squawking cries.

As they rounded a curve in the jungle path, Barker was suddenly startled to find that Farulap was walking behind him! He had not heard nor seen the little man approach. Kitson halted and greeted Farulap. Then he introduced Andrea. Farulap was carrying a bow and had a bamboo quiver full of arrows slung over one shoulder, and he said something to Philip.

"He says that with your pale skin and long white hair, you are the ugliest thing he has ever seen, Andrea. The only other thing almost as ugly, is you, James!" said Philip with a straight face as he interpreted the little man's chatter.

Andrea's eyes widened in surprise. She opened her mouth but before she could reply, Kitson let out a roar of laughter. James looked puzzled, too, and Philip explained the Islander's custom. "So," he said, "you can both take it as a compliment!"

James and Andrea both smiled and shook Farulap's hand. Then the four of them continued walking, but with the little Islander in the front. About an hour later, they entered a clearing in the jungle and saw a simple structure which reminded James and Andrea of the Parks Board picnic shelters back home in British Columbia. This one was completely open, with poles holding up a roof made from woven palm leaves. Inside, there was a large oval ring of simple benches made by fastening a pole onto two short uprights set in the dirt floor. The place was a buzz of conversation, and there were several women rocking back and forth and moaning softly. "Those are the new widows," Kitson pointed out to James and Andrea.

Philip clapped his hands and the locals gave him their attention. He spoke in their language, and there were many interjections from his listeners. Andrea was fascinated as she watched the expressions on the peoples' faces. After about twenty minutes, Philip clapped again, and the people stood to their feet. He then led them in a sort of shuffling dance, crocodile fashion, around the outside of the shelter and returned once more for them all to take their places. He spoke for a few minutes before calling Farulap to the front.

The little man chattered away in an animated voice and there were many 'clicks' and nods from his audience. All of a sudden, Farulap raised both his hands above his head, and looked up to the roof with tears streaming down his cheeks. This seemed to be some sort of signal to the others, and in moments, all but a few were doing the same!

Philip strolled over to James and Andrea and explained what had happened. "I spoke to them about the tragedy that took place yesterday." He said. "Then, I told them that the Great God of the Heavens, the One they call *The Sky God*, wants to send them what He promised, The Comforter, who is the Holy Spirit. I told them that He knows their sorrow, and that Farulap had met Him. Of course I used many illustrations, and they asked many questions, but that was basically what I taught them today. Then Farulap shared how he escaped from the monster shark, and how he met the Sky God when I prayed with him last night on the dock. He told them how he had received the Comforter. Then he simply asked them if they wanted to meet and receive the Comforter, too. The man is simply an evangelist!"

"What was the little 'Congo dance' about, around the shelter," asked Barker.

"Oh, that? That was to get the blood flowing in their rear ends again!" said Kitson with a chuckle. "Have you ever sat on anything for so long that is so hard and uncomfortable as those benches?"

"And the tears...?" asked Andrea.

"That was the beautiful part," said Philip. "Farulap had just told them his testimony, his story of how he met Christ on the dock last night when I prayed with him. And how the Holy Spirit had flooded into his own spirit, bringing peace where there had been anguish, and joy where there had been sorrow over the loss of Pikelot and his other friends. Then he told them that anyone of them that opened their own spirit to accept Christ, the Sky God's Son, would also receive the same! Many responded, and it happened to them just as he said it would. That is what the tears were about. Those were tears of joy."

Philip went back to the front of the ring of people, and spoke to them briefly. Then he walked back to James and Andrea and said, "Okay. It's time for us to go. We will leave them in Farulap's hands. They will be doing a lot of celebrating from now until late tonight."

As they strolled back to the cottage—it was much hotter now, so they ambled along, keeping to the shade—Philip spoke more on his work as a missionary to these people. "We came here three years ago," he said. "That's another story, and I was halfway through telling James yesterday, when the tragedy of the shark attack became known. Anyway, as I was saying, we came here three years ago. Dorothy and I built the clinic, and we started to learn the Islanders' language. We befriended them, and Dorothy treated the sick. They were very suspicious at first, and some were quite hostile. But eventually we won their trust.

"I waited until one of them asked me why we had come to help them, before telling them that God loved them. And I continued to wait another year before they sent a couple of spokespersons to meet with me and invite me to tell them about God. By then, and that was only four months ago, they were open and receptive to the gospel. There was also some supernatural help forthcoming from the Lord, and that 'pressed the starter button' so to speak."

Kitson, Andrea and Barker had reached a narrow path that led through a dense part of the forest, and they were forced to walk in single file. Once again, many colourful birds could be seen flying about in the trees above their heads. However, Andrea did not notice the birds. She was deep in thought, considering what Philip had been saying. She had many questions to ask, and she also wondered what James was thinking. After fifteen minutes, they were back on a wide track and were able to walk abreast of one another again.

"Just now, you mentioned something about supernatural help coming from God," she said.

"Yes," replied Philip. "It was quite amazing. Dorothy had been treating the sick for a little more than two years when the wife of the local witchdoctor brought her child to the clinic. Dorothy took one look and saw that the child was very near to death. She had been bitten by a poisonous snake three days previously, when she was playing in the jungle. Her husband, the chief witchdoctor on the island, had cast his spells and tried all of his remedies, but to no avail. In desperation, the mother had brought the child to Dorothy in the dead of night—probably to avoid the prohibitions from her husband."

"What happened?" Andrea asked.

"Dorothy awakened me, and told me how serious the case was. The child had not responded to any treatment Dorothy had tried. She was basically dead, with lung and heart paralysis from the poison. So we laid hands on her as the Bible says we should do and we prayed.

Actually, it was astonishing what happened. Both Dorothy and I had our eyes closed, and we heard the mother gasp. So we opened our eyes, and the child was breathing again. As we began to praise God, the little one opened her eyes *and sat up!* That's when the mother sat down! Suddenly! And when we handed the child to her, she just sat there and cried. Sobbed and sobbed. And we cried with her."

"What did the witchdoctor say about that?" It was James voice they heard, and Andrea could see he was fighting to keep his emotions under control.

"At first he said it was our magic. Then he wanted to worship us! I explained to him that the Sky God had done it because we worshipped Him. That was too much for the fellow. You see, he had been taught by the witchdoctors before him, and he himself had continued to teach all the people, that the Sky God was angry with His people and His creation. So, in order to survive, they had to worship the lesser gods. They were seen as 'go-betweens.' What he didn't know, was that these lesser gods are actually demons!"

James fell silent at this, and spoke no more on the rest of the way home. Andrea, however, remained very curious and was eager to hear more.

"Philip," she said, "Did the witchdoctor ever come around?"

"Yes, Andrea. His name is Farulap!"

10

The three reached the path to the cottage just as Dorothy left the clinic and they fell into step beside her.

"How did it go, Philip?" she asked.

"Oh, Dorothy, what can I say? It was amazing!" he replied. "I gave them words of comfort because of the tragedy. I explained, once again, the gospel of the Kingdom of God, and His love. There were lots of questions. Then I called Farulap to the front so that he could tell them what had happened to him. I could see that they were surprised and a little nervous at his presence. But he gave his testimony, and then an 'invitation' for salvation! Can you believe that?"

"Praise God!" spluttered Dorothy, almost choking. "How did he phrase it?"

"It was very interesting how he put it, really," said Philip. "He said, 'For many movements of the sun, and for many moons, and for many children having children, we have followed the ways that were shown to us to pay homage to the gods of the waters and the forest and fire. But we knew that the Sky God, who is above them all, was angry with us and we could not meet with him. That has now ended. The Sky God has sent his son, the one Wise-One calls Jesus, to invite us back onto the trail with him, and to help us to walk with him. He has said we must come to him, forget the lesser gods now, and put our trust in him. If we do, he will mark our names on the big tree in the sky, the tree where there is a leaf for every person who has ever lived, but whose name might not be marked on the leaf unless they accept the son's invitation. So, I'm asking you all to consider this offer from him who is above all gods. You must choose who you will worship.'"

"Incredible!" said Dorothy, "absolutely incredible."

"And about ninety percent of those that were there, perhaps seventeen or eighteen out of the twenty, responded to his invitation to meet the Sky God and receive the Comforter. *Isn't that fantastic?"*

"Praise God," said Dorothy again, "after all this time, and all your work."

"Not just mine, dear," replied Philip, as they entered the cottage. "You showed them love and care. We learned their language and their customs. We respected them as persons, and never pushed the gospel down their throats. When we had earned the right to speak, and only when they approached us, did we tell it like it is! And all the while, the Holy Spirit was softening their hearts. Then He did that healing miracle, and He revealed the Father to Farulap."

An Islander had brought a large rockfish to Dorothy shortly before she had gone up to the clinic that morning. Philip turned to James and said, "You must be an expert at preparing fish, James. What do you recommend?"

"I usually put some oil on the fish, pour lemon juice inside with salt, and pepper, and wrap it in aluminium foil. Then I put it on the barbeque. It's quite simple."

"Yes, I do have those things," replied Philip. Going to a kitchen cupboard, he rummaged around and brought several items to the counter by the sink.

"You've got almost everything we need," said Barker, "but there is one more thing. Do you have aluminium foil?"

"No," replied Kitson, "but I have discovered a substitute that the Islanders use. I'll go and get some."

Philip showed Barker where hot coals were glowing in the little pot-bellied wood stove that he always fired up every morning to run the hot water system. "Take these," he said, "and we will have our lunch much sooner! But, put several logs in the stove to keep it going for later."

Barker got the barbecue fire going nicely with a mixture of glowing coals, and some logs. Then he returned to the kitchen and prepared the fish, gutting it and removing the innards. Kitson had returned with several large green banana leaves, and Barker placed the fish on to one of the broad leaves. Then he poured the lemon juice into the inner exposed part of the fish. When he had done this, he painted the outside with the oil and sprinkled salt and pepper onto the skin. Finally, he wrapped the fish in the first leaf, and then in the second. Placing it on the grill he looked at his watch. "Five minutes each side," he said.

Andrea using one hand, helped Dorothy carry a lightweight folding table out onto the lawn in the shade of the cottage, and they pulled up some deck chairs. Then they set the cutlery and plates in place. Philip brought four plastic wine glasses and a bottle of ice-cold Zinfandel from California.

"This is a celebration!" he said enthusiastically. "We are celebrating James and Andrea's visit to this island; we are celebrating the healing that is progressing in Andrea's arm and skin; we are celebrating Farulap's conversion from witchcraft to Christ; we are celebrating my wonderful wife; we are celebrating…"

"We will be celebrating something else, soon,!" interrupted Dorothy, brandishing a large knife she had brought to cut up the fish.

They laughed heartedly and were soon tucking in to the fish, which was delicious, and which was served with some salad that

Dorothy had made.

The wine turned out to perfectly compliment the fish, and at the end of the meal, Barker raised his glass. "To you, Philip, and to you Dorothy," he toasted, "May the good Lord you serve, heap His blessings upon you!" And Andrea, quite surprised at his words, smiled to herself and drank with him.

Then Barker said to Philip, "We were interrupted yesterday when we were talking out here. I would like very much to hear the rest of your story, and I'm sure that Andrea would want to as well."

Dorothy started to rise from the table to return to the clinic, but found Philip's restraining hand on her arm. "Can you spare a few minutes?" he asked her. "Yesterday, I was sharing with James how I realized that my life was a complete sham, and a total mess, despite my whopping salary, lovely waterfront house, and invitations to speak here there and everywhere. I told him that I believed that God showed me the futility of worldly success apart from Him, and that He also spoke to me about making changes, so that I resigned from work. Then I phoned you and invited you out to lunch, after which I told you what I had done, remember? I said that you stood up at the table and said something that blew my mind! My conversation with James ended at that point, because the survivors of the shark attack arrived on the beach."

Dorothy sat down again, while Andrea and Barker leaned forward in their seats.

"I looked at the man who had neglected me and our children," she said. "I saw the man who had made many promises to change his ways and had never delivered on any of them. I saw the man who other people called Mister Success, yet both of us knew was Mister Failure. So, I stood up and said, 'I'll believe you if you sell everything and we go onto the mission field!"

11

What are you so deep in thought about, honey?" whispered Andrea as she lay next to James that night.

"It is hard for me to talk about," he replied softly. "The trouble is, partly anyway, that I'm not really sure *what* to say. A million thoughts seem to chase each other around in my mind. It's almost as though I can hear voices in my head. One says, 'What about such-and-such,' and another, answers immediately, 'Yes, but...'

"It's all to do with God, isn't it?" said Andrea.

"Yes," he replied, "at least I think so. Why is it so difficult? I mean, why can't I simply figure it all out? You know that I have always been able to figure things out. Why such a struggle with this God-issue?"

Andrea turned in his arms and faced him. She pulled his face down to hers and kissed him softly on the lips. Barker felt his blood-pressure beginning to soar, and he pulled away and sat up, breathing hard. "No, honey," he whispered as he saw the mixture of hurt and surprise on her face. "I love you! I want you! But we mustn't...anymore. Not until.... Well, not until I get things straightened out in my mind."

He turned toward her and she saw the perplexity in his expression. Reaching down, he took her hand and said quietly, but agitatedly, "Ruth's words are burning in my ears. Before we left Victoria, she confronted me, as you know. She talked to you, too, didn't she? She told me that she loved you, Andrea, that she believed that you are God's chosen mate for my life. But she said we should get married, before God and man, before we live together, before we have sex, before we just sail off."

"Yes, I know. Ruth said the same sort of things to me, and she talked about God and stuff."

"Well, I got kinda short with her. Told her I didn't believe that a marriage ceremony made a marriage. I told her the two people made the marriage. I also told her I did not believe in God. I said that my studies in astronomy had satisfied my mind that there is no god. 'God,' I said, 'was a figment of peoples' imaginations. They invented God because they couldn't explain certain things, and because they wanted some Father Figure's shoulder to cry on and look to for comfort when the going got tough....' It wasn't a good ending to our time together."

"Why don't you talk with Philip some more, James? He is such a...er...*sensible* man. Chat to him. Ask him why he believes."

He leaned down and kissed her firmly, then went to his own bed. "I love you!" she heard as he turned off the light.

Andrea lay awake thinking about the struggle James was having. She realised that she, too, had problems believing in God, but that deep down, she *almost* believed. Then when James' sister Ruth had spoken with her before they left Victoria, something had opened in her heart. Thinking about it, she wondered whether that was God trying to get through to her. Was that possible? Why would God want to bother with her, anyway? These thoughts chased themselves around in her mind until she drifted off to sleep.

Both she and Barker awakened the following morning which had dawned bright and clear, but there was a distinctly different feel to the air. At the breakfast table James mentioned this to Philip, and he nodded. "Yes," he said round a mouthful of fruit and home-made yogurt. "We are in for a change. I hope we get some rain, things are getting dry." Then he looked up at James, "Oh, I was forgetting. I guess you don't want any rain until you get that hole in your boat fixed?"

"Right," agreed Barker. "I will hurry down and start on the stern after breakfast. Honey, can you help me today?"

"Sure," said Andrea. "There's only so much I can do with one arm, but don't you want to make enquiries about those guard rails?"

"I do, but they can wait for a while. What I really want to do is fix the stern before the rain comes, and you can help by passing things to me when I need them."

Barker and Andrea were down at the yacht within about fifteen minutes, and James was pleased to see Philip turn up to help. The sky was still clear, but the breeze had shifted from east to the south. All three began with sanding and smoothing away the broken fragments around the gaping hole which measured fully two feet in length and varied in width from five to twelve inches. James had run the yacht's engine to supply electrical power and he was able to do the rougher spots with his electric disc sander. Andrea worked slowly using only one hand. They were finished in less than an hour.

Then James and Andrea donned face masks and rubber gloves, and Philip watched them apply resin and carefully cut pieces of fibreglass woven cloth over the hole. The trickiest part was when James laid cloth from the inside of the stern, but he managed by contorting himself and working from below the cockpit and behind the engine.

An hour later, the resin had set and another layer was applied. By mid morning clouds had gathered, and were shielding them from the direct sunlight. This was a blessing, and they continued working until after one thirty. The hole was sealed off, and the third layer of glass and resin was setting.

"It looks rough right now," said Barker, "but I can sand it smooth later. At least we have been able to do this before the rains, and it is sealed up now, with the backstay fitting attached again."

"Time for a cuppa," suggested Philip, "and, maybe a bite to eat?"

Locking up the yacht once more, Barker followed Andrea and Kitson up to the cottage. "I recommend that we all take a shower soon, to wash off the deposit of fine fibreglass particles and dust. Otherwise, it will probably cause our skin to itch pretty soon."

"How about a swim, first?" suggested Andrea. "I've been longing to take a dip in the sea, here. It looks so inviting."

"Okay," replied Philip, "a swim sounds like a great first step to cooling down, and ridding ourselves of skin irritants!"

Five minutes later, Philip led the way to the beach in front of the cottage. "This is better for swimming," he said. "The lagoon by the dock is where the fishermen clean their fish, and it is not as clean as down here."

Their dip in the ocean was indeed pleasant and refreshing. Andrea had sealed the plaster cast on her arm using two plastic bags and an elastic band. But the weather was changing rapidly and the wind had picked up. Dark clouds promised rain and by the time they had reached the cottage, large drops were falling.

Inside the cottage, James Barker was restless. Clad only in his bathing shorts, he stood at the living room window and watched the rain storm grow in intensity. He was worried about his boat, wondering whether it was moored securely enough at the dock.

"Philip," he called, "What sort of rain storms do you have in these parts? Do the winds and seas become violent?"

Kitson, who had taken a quick shower and changed into some clothes, sensed Barker's anxiety, and joined him at the window. "We do get some very violent storms here," he said. "Are you worried about your boat?"

"Yes," replied Barker. "I should have secured her with spring lines.... I think I had better run down and do that now."

He turned and hurried to the spare room, where he found Andrea collecting her clothes before taking a shower. He told her what he was going to do, and left the cottage, running through the heavy rain.

Naked from the waist up, Barker felt the sting of the large raindrops on his face and shoulders. Visibility in the tropical downpour was almost zero, and he had to exercise great caution to negotiate the steps to the dock. *One slip,* he thought to himself...

Reaching the dock, he hurried to the Robson, and found her straining at her mooring lines and surging back and forth. He was just in time and was glad he had decided to secure the boat with spring lines. Climbing into the cockpit, he found the wildly bucking motion quite a hindrance to opening the locker in which his extra mooring lines were stashed. Eventually he had three separate woven Dacron lines and two additional fenders on the pitching dock and he went to work. It was twenty minutes before he had secured the Robson to his satisfaction, all the while working in what seemed to him to be under a waterfall! Barker had never experienced such rain before. It simply cascaded down out of the skies.

Shielding his eyes with one hand, and balancing himself on the rolling dock, he weaved his way back to the steps like a drunken sailor. Rainwater flowed down off his head and torso in small rivers and he realized he would not need to take a shower at the cottage. The salt water from his swim in the sea had been washed away thoroughly, and he smiled at the thought. Mounting the steps carefully, he turned at the top to check how the boat was behaving with the two spring lines fore and aft, and the extra beam line he had attached to the dock. It was difficult to get a good sighting in the pouring rain. However, between violent gusts of wind, he could see that the boat was no longer surging like a race horse waiting to explode out of the starting enclosure. He had done all he could, so he turned and struggled back to the cottage battered by wind and rain.

Philip and Andrea had eaten lunch and Barker found them in the lounge chatting. Andrea looked up as he walked in. "Wow!" she exclaimed, jumping up and rushing to fetch him a towel. "I'll fix you something to eat, while you get some clothes on."

When Barker returned to the kitchen table, he found a huge sandwich made from a thawed-out and micro-waved super bun. Andrea had loaded its insides with chunks of tinned ham, mustard, ketchup, and dark coloured leaves that Philip had shown her. "Dorothy's locally grown spinach," he had said. He filled a mug with tea and carried his lunch through to join the others. "Do you run a generator for power?" he asked Kitson, and then began eating while Philip replied.

"Yes, we brought one with us. Dorothy wanted a microwave for some of her medical work, so we figured electrical power for the cottage and clinic was a must. It has been a real blessing. We decided that with a little bit of planning, we could maintain a high standard of comfort. Things like a bath or shower, with hot water—that's what the little wood stove is for. But for the kitchen, for washing the dishes, and the laundry, and for the hospital, the generator provides the power for lighting, and for the hot water tank. You know," he continued, "we felt that although we had chosen to live in the 'boonies', with a little effort we could still be civilized."

Andrea put down her mug and turned toward Kitson. "Philip, she said, "did you build this house and the clinic all by yourself?"

"Well, not exactly," he replied. "We do not belong to an official missions organisation, we wanted to come without strings, if you know what I mean. But we planned this move very carefully. I told you that I was an accountant, remember?" He looked at her and she nodded in understanding.

"Well, most accountants are careful, cautious, people. I sold our fancy home and the two vehicles we owned, and we took a trip out here. Dorothy had been looking into mission work for some time, I discovered. We flew to Manila and I found a chap who had a large diesel cruiser and that he ferried people and supplies out to the Caroline Islands. Dorothy had her heart fixed on Truk Island, since there was no clinic here, and so we camped for one week while our ferry unloaded stuff at other islands.

"During that week we realized what we would need regarding a home, a clinic, and the support things like power, water and sewage disposal facilities. I returned two months later with a builder friend who had retired and wanted some excitement. Together, we made a start on the two buildings, and the dock. He also helped me with constructing the septic tanks and the hot water system. We spent three months here, and by the end of that time, the Islanders—locals—had become more friendly. They were very shy at first, I hardly saw them. Once the dock was built, and they discovered that I had made it for them to use, my relationship with them began to progress rapidly.

"I returned with Dorothy—she had finished up her work with a clinic back home—and we continued with the finishing touches to the cottage and the clinic. I should say *finishing labour*, what a lot there was still to do! Anyway, that's my long-winded answer to both of your questions."

"And on-going supplies, Philip?" asked Andrea.

"I can call a chap in Ponape by radio," Philip replied, "and a boat calls by once a month and drops off stuff at these islands. And that way, we can even get some luxury items, frozen, of course, and we keep them in our deep freeze."

The wind had eased but the rain was still falling heavily. Barker glanced at his watch and saw that it was three-o-five. "Let's get some letters written," he said to Andrea, so they excused themselves for the afternoon.

12

While Barker, and Andrea (with some difficulty) were writing letters to family and friends back home in British Columbia, Philip Kitson braved the heavy rain and went to see how Dorothy was getting on at the clinic. His legs were quite wet from the scant protection provided by his umbrella, but the air was warm and he felt little discomfort. Dorothy was busy dressing the nasty-looking wound a child had received when a rock fell on his leg. The boy had been playing on a stretch of beach where the rocks were jagged and sharp. He had fallen and dislodged a big rock which had slashed his leg as it fell past him into the rock-pools below.

Dorothy had applied some local anaesthetic, had cleaned the wound, and was busy putting stitches in place when Philip arrived. Immediately he helped her by cleaning up and disposing of left over pieces of bandage and used swabs. When the boy had left—the rain did not seem to bother the islanders—and Dorothy had given extra painkillers to his mother who was with him, she suggested that Philip might make them some tea.

They sat together in her little office at one end of the clinic. To one side were two small 'surgical areas', and beyond those, a space that served as a clean-up area, cum-tearoom-cum-drug storage room, and little wash room. A door led from this room into a large area partially divided across the middle. There were two beds in each half, and were there for patients who needed to stay over night or for a longer period. All in all it was a very handy and practical little clinic and was serving the medical needs of the island, well.

As Philip and Dorothy sipped their tea, and watched the rain still pouring down, he said, "I think that James has seen some things that have started him thinking."

"Yes," replied Dorothy. "When I was talking with Andrea in the kitchen yesterday, I could see that she has a very soft heart. She really loves James. And I also see a gentle side to him, he's not inconsiderate at all. Have you noticed how he always cares for Andrea's needs?"

Philip nodded. "I think we should pray for both of them."

Bowing their heads, they entered into a time of intercession for James and Andrea, completely unaware that their prayers echoed those that Linda Barker and her daughter Ruth had offered up to God many thousands of miles away.

Some time after five that afternoon, the skies cleared and the wind died down to a gentle whisper. Andrea had finished two letters; one was to her parents, and the other to James' sister, Ruth. Andrea had described the shark attack and her broken arm, as well as the wonderful blessing of finding medical treatment and excellent hospitality in such a remote place as Truk Island.

Barker had written to his parents and he had told them about their adventures in the crossing from Hawaii to the Caroline Islands, ending with the attack from the Great White shark. He had concluded his letter with a brief account of the shark attack on the local fishermen, and the kindness and hospitality he and Andrea had received from the Kitsons. He had sat for a long time deliberating whether or not to mention the episode with Farulap, or to relay some of Philip Kitson's testimony. In the end he had decided not to tackle either subject. He didn't quite know why, but he did not feel comfortable writing about 'God things' as he called them.

Barker noticed the change in weather first. He walked to the window in the lounge and looked out on a sparkling sea. Then he went over to where Andrea was putting the final words down on her second letter, and he bent down and nuzzled her on the side of her neck. She shivered and he saw the goose bumps rise on her arm. Grinning, he said, "Do you want to come for a walk with me down to the boat?"

"In a minute, yes," she said, "Just let me finish this. It'll only take me a moment."

Then they left, hand in hand, and strolled down to the steps, marvelling at how fresh and clean everything looked after the rain. Despite the very heavy downpour, there were no pools of rainwater lying around. Reaching the Robson, Barker noted with satisfaction that she had not popped her fenders when the strong winds had buffeted her. They climbed on board and he unlocked the cabin. Down below, they tidied up and put all the loose items of clothing, charts, and kitchen-ware away in the appropriate lockers. When everything was ship-shape, Barker pulled Andrea down onto his lap on the saloon settee. They smooched for a while, and then he moved her off his lap and onto the seat.

Taking a kneeling position in front of her, Barker held both of Andrea's hands, and she noticed that he was very careful and gentle with the arm that was encased in plaster. Then he looked into her eyes for a long moment.

"You are incredibly beautiful, my darling," he said softly. "Andrea, I love you." His eyes searched her face, and he saw the lovely curve of her mouth with the lips slightly parted. "I want to thank you for being with me, for coming with me on this wild adventure."

She was silent, and simply looked at him, her eyes not leaving his. Then she heard him say her name once more.

"Andrea...honey...will you marry me?"

She sat there, stunned, not knowing what to say. Then for answer, she loosened her hands from his, and reached out, taking his face and pulling it toward her. Her lips parted, and she kissed him for a long moment. Then she leaned back a little and simply nodded. It was only when Barker felt he was about to drown in those big, beautiful eyes, that he heard her whispered reply, "Yes."

He stayed where he was, kneeling at her feet, and they simply held on to each other. There was no need for further conversation, and a sense of great peace enveloped them both.

Several minutes later, Barker stood up and helped Andrea to her feet. This time, she took his hands and said softly, "James, tell me what you are thinking. Where, and how, are we to get married? Remember how we talked before? You said marriage was…." She stopped because his finger was across her mouth.

"Shhh," he whispered. "Something inside of me has happened. I know I said marriage was an outdated practice, but I did not know what I was talking about. I'm sorry, now, that I said those words. I've been doing a lot of thinking, and I just *know* that we must get married. There is a right way to do things. Ruth was right on when she confronted me in Victoria." He continued, "Honey, Philip is a minister, or a priest, or something. I think we should talk to him about it, and ask him if he will marry us!"

Then, arm in arm, they went up to the cottage. Dorothy had the kitchen table set, and a large steak and kidney pie thawed and heating up in the microwave. Philip had sliced up a plate full of sugar mangoes from the trees which grew in profusion on the island. It was a delightful combination, the sweet fruit complimenting the strong savoury flavour of the pie. When they had finished their meal, James insisted on doing the washing up, and the others went through to the lounge.

When he had poured his tea, he joined them and sat with Andrea on the sofa. After a lull in the conversation, Barker took Andrea's hand and turned to Philip and Dorothy. Clearing his throat, he said, "Philip, Dorothy, there is something I want to tell you."

All of a sudden he felt embarrassed, and was at a loss for words. Then Andrea squeezed his hand, and leaning forward, she kissed his cheek. He recovered his composure, and continued. "Philip, Dorothy…Andrea and I want to get married. I proposed to her this afternoon, and she accepted! I—er—that is…"

What ever else he was about to say was drowned out by Philip's, and Dorothy's loud cries of joy. They both jumped to their feet and stood on either side of James and Andrea on the sofa.

"Congratulations…Wonderful…Praise God!…" were some of the exclamations the couple heard. Then James looked up at Philip and said, "Do you mind if we talk with you two about this, about marriage?"

Philip quickly pulled the two chairs that Dorothy and he were sitting on, closer to the sofa. "Yes—I mean no—I mean, go right ahead."

James shuffled his feet and replied, "Today, this afternoon, during the rain storm, a strange feeling came over me. I can't describe it really, it's just that I suddenly *knew* that Andrea and I should get married, that it was the right thing to do. So, I asked her to go down to the Robson with me when the rain stopped. We cleaned up inside, and then I—er—I asked her to marry me…and she accepted. After a while, we talked a bit, I told Andrea that it was right for us to be married, and that if it was possible, to discuss it with you." He saw Philip about to speak, and he quickly continued.

"Philip, you are a priest or a missionary or something, aren't you? Will you marry us? And will you be a witness, Dorothy?" His words came out in a rush.

It was very quiet in the cottage lounge after James had finished speaking. Then Philip answered. "James and Andrea, Dorothy and I are so happy for the two of you in this decision. So, I want to answer 'yes' to your request for me to conduct the marriage. But I also have to answer 'no' at the same time. Please listen to me carefully.

"Dorothy and I are what the Bible calls 'born again' Christians. We believe very strongly in the sanctity of marriage, and of the family as God's very first 'organisation', or institution. I am qualified under United States Law to conduct a marriage ceremony between two consenting adults. I think that my qualification is recognized in Canada, but these islands are under U.S. jurisdiction, anyway. Now, I believe that there are two equally important parts to a marriage. One part is before God; the other is before Man.

"The part before Man involves what the Bible terms *'rendering to Caesar what is due to Caesar.'* This means that a country's laws need to be obeyed, the rules adhered to, the fees and taxes paid, the paper-work properly completed. Most countries have such laws concerning marriages; some are very loose about things, but generally, there are always some legalities attached to marriage. This is the 'Caesar' part.

"But the most important part of a marriage from the Christian viewpoint, is the 'God part.' Dorothy and I, and most serious Christians, really believe that. We believe that the Bible reveals that God established the marriage relationship, one man to one woman, for life. In the second chapter of the book of Genesis, it says that *a man shall leave his parents and shall cleave to his wife; and they shall become one flesh.* The cleaving part, and the one flesh part, refer to the importance of establishing a separate family unit, and to sexual union. When a man and a woman have sexual intercourse, they cleave, and they become one flesh. In one sense, they become 'married' in the sight of God. We believe that Jesus confirmed this view, and that the Holy Spirit led the apostle Paul to write that sexual intimacy in marriage is a shadow of Christ's desire for intimacy with His Church—the Universal Church of all believers of all time—and that is why His church is called His Bride.

"So, I want very much for both of you, James, and Andrea, to understand what you have asked me to do in marrying you. You are asking me, and Dorothy as a witness, *to bring you before God and agree with your vows of commitment to each other.* We both feel very honoured, and very privileged, to have been asked to do this. But I have felt it necessary to inform you of our views on marriage, that is why I said *yes, and no,* to give you the opportunity to think it over before you make a final decision.

"So, I have a suggestion. Please consider what I have said and discuss it together, and we will talk about it tomorrow. Is that acceptable to you both?"

When Philip had finished speaking, he took Dorothy's hand, they said good night to James and Andrea, and left for their bedroom. James looked at Andrea, and shrugged. "What do you think about all that, honey?" he asked.

Andrea was still for a moment. Then she replied, surprised at her own boldness. "James, I think I agree with everything that Philip said. I have always thought that 'marriage' is for life, and that somehow, God is involved, or at least holds it high on His list." She looked intently at him before adding, "And darling, I love you. I want to spend my life with you. That's why I have come away with you on this adventure."

James was looking at the floor, and was deep in thought. "Yes," he said at length, "I feel the same way about you. And you heard what he said about sexual intimacy. We have made love often. I have felt some sort of 'connection,' some sort of *joining,* at those times. Now, I think I understand what the cleaving, and one flesh bit, is about... I guess that in God's sight, we are already married, but at the same time, not exactly in the proper way. Am I making sense?"

"Perfectly," she said, "let's talk about it some more, with Philip, in the morning. I'm tired, can we go to bed?"

13

The next morning, when James and Andrea entered the kitchen for breakfast, there was a note for them on the table. Philip had written, *A good morning to you both! Please help yourselves to breakfast. Dorothy has gone up to the clinic to attend to a sick woman, and Farulap appeared early at the cottage and said there were large numbers of Islanders gathered at the shelter and waiting for me to come and explain 'things about God' to them. I should be back by noon.*

For some reason he could not explain, Barker felt a sense of relief at not having to discuss the marriage issue with Philip, or even Andrea. He had lain awake for hours wrestling with his thoughts before finally falling asleep after midnight. In the morning, during and after his shower, the 'voices' in his mind had started up once again. Then, after he had read Philip's note, he felt relieved.

For her part as well, Andrea was not at peace. Her thrill and inner joy which had come when James had proposed to her on the yacht, had been replaced by a feeling of unrest. She had woken up quite early that morning, and she had gone over in her mind all that Philip had said. Andrea knew that the essence of his conversation lined up with what Ruth had shared with her before their voyage had begun. What puzzled her was something she perceived going on with James.

Her intuition told her that something was amiss, something was not quite right, and that it was important for that 'something' to be resolved. She was also aware that deep down, she herself needed to bring her relationship, or connection, with God, into some sort of closure, or settlement.

They prepared and ate their breakfast in silence, each pondering their thoughts, and each one, initially, unaware of the lack of conversation between them. It was Barker who first noticed that neither of them had spoken during breakfast. He looked at Andrea and said, "Hey, honey! We are both very quiet this morning. What are you thinking about?"

She shook her head, her mouth full of cereal, and he waited. "Just...about what Philip said last night...and...you know, *marriage.*"

Barker pushed his empty bowl away and sipped his coffee. Then he said, "I've got those 'voices' going big time in my head this morning. I'm glad, in one sense, that we are alone...that Philip was called away." He was silent for a while. Then, "There is something that I *must* come to grips with, but the problem is that I don't really know what it is! All I know is that I don't believe in God!" and he pushed his coffee mug away from himself so violently that half of it spilled on the table.

Andrea looked at him, saw his perplexity, and her heart went out to him. She wished she could help him, but knew on the inside that she, too, was trying to come to grips with that elusive 'something.' Instead, she went over to the kitchen sink and fetched a dishcloth which she handed to him.

James wiped up his coffee spill and then suddenly stood up from the table. "I want to take *Skipping Stone* out for a short sail this morning to test the backstay repair job. Do you want to come?"

"Can you do the tests by yourself?" Andrea asked, "I would like to stay here, be quiet, and think about things."

"No problem," Barker replied. "I should only be about one to two hours at the most." With that he left for the dock and got the yacht ready for the ocean. In fifteen minutes the sails had been set for raising into position once they cleared the shallows, and he had backed *Skipping Stone* away from the dock. The Robson swung around sharply under power and Barker steered her out into the deeper waters of the lagoon. Then he went forward and raised the working jib, leaving the sail loose and flapping in the breeze.

Returning to the cockpit, he loosened the mainsail halyard from its cleat and cranked the big sail up the mast. Then he tightened the jib sheets and remembered, with a smile, Andrea's confusion over terms such as sheets and halyards for ropes, when he had first introduced her to sailing. Finally, with both sails pulling beautifully, he turned off the engine and settled down, joyful as the yacht surged through the swells in the deep water. Revelling in the near perfect sailing conditions, he closed his eyes and let his body connect with the rhythm of his world, the boat and the sea moving together in concert.

This is it, he said to himself, *yes, this is where I find my peace.*

His thoughts wandered but returned suddenly to his problem. *God! Did, or does, God exist? 'Of course not,' shrieked one voice in his head, to which another replied, 'You know He does, James!'* He shook his head and forcibly cleared his thoughts by focussing on the rhythm of the waves on the motion of his yacht, anticipating each change in balance as *Skipping Stone* danced peacefully along.

Ten minutes later, he opened his eyes and pulled the tiller toward him. At the same time, he slackened the mainsail sheets and then did the same for the jib. The boom swung out until it was almost at ninety degrees to his line of direction, and *Skipping Stone* straightened up as she slipped through the water, running down wind. This was the moment of testing. Barker turned to see how the backstay fitting, in its thick bedding of new fibreglass, was holding out. All was well, and he held course. Relaxing back at the tiller, Barker once more felt his whole being getting in tune with the ocean. *Running before the wind, is so different from reaching across the wind or beating into it,* he thought lazily. The Robson swayed slowly from side to side as she accelerated down one side of the following swells and then slowed down in the troughs as her bow ploughed into the wave ahead. Lashing the tiller, he clambered past the dinghy and went to the foredeck. Grasping the forestay in one hand, he leaned out and had an uninterrupted view of the ocean ahead. He saw that the Robson was bearing down on Little Truk Island, and he remembered from his charts that there were hidden reefs in the vicinity. So, he hurried back to the cockpit and brought the boat's bow around and across the wind. Resetting the sails, he sat back once more and closed his eyes.

A little over a mile from *Skipping Stone,* and at a depth of seventy five feet beneath the surface, a dramatic change took place on and around the reef. All the colourful rockfish and the schools of silvery mackerel suddenly vanished. A large grouper backed under a ledge and remained even more motionless than normal, only its eyes moving as it surveyed its surrounds for danger. A dozen or more parrot-fish dived for shelter into nooks and crannies and waited for the gigantic predator to pass.

The Great White had not caught a substantial fish since his meal of fishermen a few days previously. He was hungry, and his eyes searched for any unwary grouper that might be wandering along the reef, itself looking for a meal. But the shark was out of luck. With a flick of its powerful tail, it swam up closer to the surface, its body twisting from side to side, alert for any signals relaying the message of food on the way. Suddenly a signal came. Something large was moving on the surface, not too far away. The Great White tuned into the message and went to investigate.

The morning breeze was pushing the Robson along on a broad

reach at a steady five knots. Apart from the lazy swells which rolled across the boat's course, lifting it and gently lowering it with a sleep-inducing motion, all was remarkably peaceful and still. Barker yawned, and leaned forward to brush a fly off his leg. *Amazing,* he thought, *all the way out here, a fly...*

In Victoria, British Columbia, it was four o'clock in the afternoon and a light rain was falling. Linda Barker hurried from her car up to the entrance of the apartment block where her daughter Ruth lived. She was in a hurry for two reasons. The first was because of the rain. But the second reason was the *real* reason she was hurrying.

Just that morning, she and Ruth had met to pray. It had been a productive time, Linda thought, and once again she and Ruth had prayed intensely for James and Andrea. However, upon reaching home, *after* they had prayed, Linda felt a tremendous burden come upon her for James. For a while she resisted the thoughts—they were all about danger, gloom, and darkness—and she figured they were simply the work of the kingdom of darkness, trying to make her anxious and worried.

But soon she realized that the Holy Spirit was burdening her so that she would intercede some more. After making lunch for her husband, she went to her bedroom and began to pray. But the burden did not lift. Eventually, she picked up the telephone and called Ruth.

"Ruth, love," she said, "I have been wrestling with a terrific burden for James ever since I arrived home. I started out resisting it; then I realized God had given it to me, so I've been interceding. The burden has not lifted. I feel I must come over and pray with you again. Is that possible? Are you very busy?"

Ruth not only understood, but she was actually eager to enter into spiritual warfare, joining with her mother to stand against the forces of evil. So, her response was, "Come right over, Mom. Let's get to work."

When the front entrance door buzzed Ruth let her mother in and in a few moments they were seated together in her living room. Linda described her feelings again, and emphasized that she felt there was a danger issue to pray about. "James is in danger, or about to enter into grave danger. I feel sure this is what the Lord is impressing on me. Satan wants to kill James, and maybe Andrea, too. I believe that the devil knows that both of them are seeking for truth, and perhaps they are close to finding it."

"I don't have that burden, Mom," said her daughter. "But, I will stand with you and pray with you until it lifts!"

Without further discussion, they began to pray. It was Linda who spoke out first, and unusually for her, she prayed pacing up and down, back and forth in the living room.

The two prayer warriors continued to pray for more than an hour, and suddenly Linda found that the burden had lifted from her shoulders. She told Ruth, and they both rejoiced. Then Linda went home.

14

A few miles off Little Truk Island in the Carolines, fifteen feet below the Robson and from thirty feet behind, the shark had seen the thing that it had encountered several days before. A tiny message glowed in the creature's brain cells, and it remembered: *No success from charging the craft; only sore teeth; lots more success from leaping upon these things.*

Focussing all its energy on the anticipated meal that lay only moments ahead, the Great White rushed forward. When its nose was about five feet from the stern of the Robson it burst forth from the ocean like a performing killer whale. Hurtling up over the remaining stubs of the stern railings it had destroyed in its previous attack, the giant shark seemed to hang in the air for a brief second before crashing down onto the cockpit of the yacht.

It was during that brief second that the roughly twenty gallons of sea and spray swept up with the giant fish flooded on board drenching the stunned and totally shocked sailor at the tiller. Barker, already leaning forward and about to swat the fly on his leg, was knocked halfway down into the cockpit well by the force of this deluge. He was momentarily aware of the sun's rays being blocked out by a huge shape just above his head, and then the weight of the falling shark hurled him onto the cockpit sole. The enormous right pectoral fin of the shark tore the newly repaired backstay out of the Robson's stern and the yacht veered sharply to starboard, heeling right over under the colossal weight that had so suddenly come upon it. The belly of the fish pulverized the tiller, snapping Barker's left leg like a twig against the side of the rudder mount. His face was thrust viciously down against the teak grid on the cockpit sole and in the midst of his agonizing pain, he was conscious of water closing over his head and almost covering his body. The built-in human survival instinct caused him to hold his breath until he thought his lungs would burst.

Fortunately for Barker, two forces working in harmony saved him from drowning. The first was the sideways thrashing and wriggling of the shark as it sought to get back into the sea. The second was that this was causing the sharply heeling yacht to lean over even further towards the other, or port, side. All the water that had gushed on board with the shark drained rapidly away from his face which faced upwards to starboard. He was able to exhale and gulp a mouthful of air.

Under the gyrations of the shark, the boom struck the surface of the sea and the boat swung around to port. As the Robson straightened up for a moment, the mast whipped forward under the combined forces of pressure from the wind, now coming from behind, and the massive jolting from the shark as it tried to free itself. This caused the mast to snap eight feet above the boom gooseneck and crash down onto the cabin roof.

The huge fish was getting desperate in its attempts to return to the ocean. Swinging its head to one side while its tail-end whipped the other way, it was doing serious damage to the yacht's super structure. As the brute's head smashed the cabin hatch to smithereens, it was biting at everything within reach of those massive teeth. These bites were having the same effect that chainsaws in the hands of demented loggers would have on the side of a log cabin that they wanted to demolish. With one huge gyration of its body, the shark finally freed itself and plunged overboard. This caused the yacht to rock wildly for a few moments before it settled down and began drifting toward Hall Island.

On the cockpit floor, Barker slowly came to his senses. His face ached from being forced against the teak grid, and his nose was broken. His right arm had gone completely numb from being jammed under his body by the combined weight of the shark and his own body. But by far, the most agonizing pain was coming from his left leg. Tasting blood, Barker raised his torso and tried to sit up. Excruciating pains lanced up his thigh and he gritted his teeth, as a wave of darkness flooded over his senses.

He sank back onto the cockpit sole for a minute. Then he tried again, more slowly and carefully. The pain was almost unbearable, but he made it to a sitting position and looked down at his leg. What he saw did not fully register for a moment. Then he realized that both his tibia and fibula had broken and that sharp and jagged ends of both bones were protruding through his skin, leaving his foot dangling at an awkward angle below. The wound was bleeding profusely into the cockpit well, and he groaned.

Barker knew that he should try to stop the flow of blood from his leg. He found a handkerchief in his right pocket, and with trembling fingers, tied it as tightly as he could, around his thigh, just above the knee. Then, reaching down onto the cockpit floor he retrieved a piece of the shattered tiller. This he pushed under the handkerchief and twisted it, making a crude tourniquet.

After a few minutes, he looked around at the devastation caused by the Great White shark. At first glance, he thought his beautiful boat was a write-off. The damage was indeed substantial. But then, he remembered that he still had an engine. Using all his strength, he hopped to the cabin steps where he could reach the tangle of shroud cables, boom and mainsail. Although the broken mast protruded beyond the bow of the yacht, he was relieved to see that none of the sails nor cables were trailing overboard. He gritted his teeth and hopped back to the center of the cockpit where a side locker housed his emergency tools. Finding the adjustable wrench, he managed to tighten it onto the stub of the rudder stock. It worked. He could steer his boat.

Then, his shaking fingers found the controls to start the engine and on the third attempt, it coughed into life. The pain and shock of his ordeal nearly overcame him at that point, and he had to sit gasping for a few minutes. Then, very slowly, he reached down and pushed the lever forward to engage the gear. The boat responded and began to move forward. With the wrench substituting as a tiller, he nosed the bow of the Robson around and headed back to Big Truk Island.

Dorothy Kitson returned to the cottage that morning shortly after Barker had backed the Robson away from the dock. She made herself a cup of tea, and toast, having missed breakfast, and carried these through to the lounge where she found Andrea looking at an old magazine from the bookshelf.

"Hi Andrea, would you like a cuppa?" she asked.

Andrea looked up and smiled. "Oh, good morning Dorothy, yes, but I will get it. You sit down and I'll join you in a minute."

The two women chatted for a while, and Dorothy was informed about James testing the repair made to the mast's backstay. Then Dorothy excused herself to return to the clinic once more. "I'll be back for lunch," she said, "and so will Philip. We can open some canned fruit to compliment the rest of the mangoes we have. Does that sound good?"

"Delicious," replied Andrea, "But let me prepare the meal. I can also bake a pan-bread to go with it if you like?"

"Sounds like just what this doctor ordered," said Dorothy

smiling, and she stepped out of the cottage.

Andrea continued reading for about an hour, and then began rummaging around in the kitchen, looking for flour, salt, and baking powder. Successful, she then mixed the required quantities of the dry materials and set the mixture aside and went looking for the tinned fruit. Soon she had located a can of pears and a can of peaches. Glancing at the digital clock on the stove, she saw that the time was eleven eighteen. "Hmm," she murmured, "I wonder what's keeping James?"

At that moment Philip arrived, hot and thirsty from walking back from the meeting in the forest shelter. Andrea noticed his condition and had a tall glass of cold water poured for him in a moment. Philip sighed and said, "What it is to be waited on hand and foot! And what will I do when you sail off into the blue?"

"Talking of sailing," said Andrea, "James took the Robson for a short sail to test the repair to the backstay. He should have been home long ago!"

The two of them walked over to the lounge windows and looked out on the beautiful view of the sea and sky. It was Philip who caught sight of the strange looking craft that was approaching the entrance to the channel through the reef. "What on earth is that...Oh...Good Lord!" he cried, "James has had an accident!"

He pointed to the stricken Robson slowly motoring towards the island. In the next moment, both Kitson and Andrea were rushing out of the cottage and down to the dock. They arrived just as Barker, on the verge of collapse, hit the side of the dock in a very rough approach.

"Oh God!" cried Andrea, "James is hurt!"

Philip caught hold of the badly dented pulpit and held on while he shouted to Andrea to switch off the engine. She leapt on board and as she bent down to disengage the gear, and turn off the motor, she saw James' leg with the bones protruding into broad daylight, and froze!

"Oh my God! Oh *darling,"* she sobbed, "Oh my poor darling!" But Barker did not hear her. The accumulation of pain, and shock, and weariness from fighting off fainting spells as he motored back to Truk Island, had finally overcome him. He had slumped down on the cockpit seat, unconscious.

Andrea was dimly aware that someone was shouting loudly nearby. Looking up, white-faced, she realized that Philip was struggling to hold the Robson with the engine going! "Switch off the engine!" he shouted for the tenth time. In a stupor, Andrea complied, and Philip was able to pull the yacht around and tie her to the dock using the single beam line that James had left there.

"Oh Lord!" said Philip, when he climbed on board to where Andrea was sitting, frozen in shock at the sight of Barker's leg. "Oh Lord!" he said again, as he looked at the devastation all around him. Then he recovered. "Quick," he said, "Andrea... *Andrea!* Come on girl, we've got to get James up to the clinic as soon as possible. Help me lift him."

Together, they tried lifting Barker, but he was a dead weight and with Andrea using only one arm, they were unable to. "Andrea, listen to me! You must go quickly to the clinic and tell Dorothy what has happened. I will stay here with James and see that he doesn't fall down and damage his leg further. *Hurry!"*

She shook her head, and then stood up, coming to her senses. "Yes," she said, and hurried off.

The two women were back at the yacht within five minutes, with one of the islanders helping Dorothy carry the stretcher. Andrea was helping by carrying the doctor's bag. Climbing onto the yacht, Dorothy quickly and calmly took charge.

"Philip, roll up his sleeve. Hold this... Wipe there... Now, hold this."

Then she took out some scissors, and cut James' trouser leg

away to expose the broken leg from the thigh down. She looked at the wound very carefully, while Barker slept on, the powerful drugs she had administered keeping him sedated. "Hmnn..." she said quietly, "This one *might* require more than I have got available...well, Andrea, Philip, bring that stretcher, and we will have to strap him on and lug him up to the clinic."

Even with the extra help from the islander, that turned out to be easier said than done, but after much struggle at the steps, they reached the top and hurried to the clinic. Dorothy had Barker placed on one of the 'surgery' beds and she went over his whole body very carefully. When she had done this she said, "A serious double-bone break on the lower left leg; a broken nose; lacerations to his back and his face; possible internal injuries. Now," she said, turning to Philip and Andrea, "wash your hands, put on those gowns, and help me!"

15

Doctor Dorothy Kitson and her two helpers worked on James Barker for a little over two hours. Philip Kitson had helped his wife on many occasions and he had become accustomed to the sights and smells of a surgical operation. Andrea Jensen, on the other hand, had hardly ever visited a hospital. She and her family and friends had enjoyed good health and had lived lives remarkably free from accidents. And so, for her, it was a traumatic experience.

Just to help remove Barker's clothes, and to clean his lacerations, was bad enough. But there was worse to come. She had watched as Dorothy had examined her 'fiancée probing his stomach and listening with her stethoscope, and that had seemed to Andrea to be quite 'normal.' But when Dorothy had asked her to pass a small hard rubber mallet, and then had struck James' nose three times, she had recoiled in horror. But Dorothy had instructed her to wipe up the blood which flowed freely after she had used the mallet, and then she had skilfully reshaped Barker's nose!

The worst part was the surgery on James' broken right leg. White faced throughout the whole ordeal, Andrea almost collapsed as she saw Dorothy make a five inch incision on one side of James' shin. The sight of the broken bones, all the blood, and worst of all the *flesh*, which Dorothy seemed to cut in the same way that Andrea had seen a butcher doing, was simply too much for her sensitive nature. She felt the nausea and her stomach heaved. Tearing off her face mask, she turned and vomited onto the cement floor. Then she staggered to a chair and slumped down, her stomach still heaving. After a few minutes, she went to the small bathroom in the cleaning up room and vomited again.

Back in the surgery, Dorothy, with Philip helping, had reset the two broken bones which despite their jagged appearance, had come together nicely. The wound was then cleaned and stitched, and Philip injected several drugs to promote healing, fight infection, and control blood clotting. He was helping Dorothy move James onto the stretcher again, when Andrea reappeared with a bucket and mop and began to clean up the mess around the surgery table.

The Kitsons carried Barker to one of the beds in the tiny hospital, and carefully covered him with a light blanket. His tightly bandaged leg was raised on several pillows, and Dorothy checked his pulse once again. She seemed satisfied, and turned away, removing her mask and gloves and stripping off her gown as she made her way back to her office. Philip also removed his gown, gloves and mask, but dumped them temporarily on the floor. Then he pulled up a chair and sat near James' bed.

He was joined by Andrea ten minutes later, and she handed him a cup of tea. "That was a new experience for you, wasn't it?" he said, after thanking her for the beverage.

Andrea nodded and he noticed that she was still rather pale. He patted her arm in encouragement and said, "You did well back there, you held out for much longer than I did the first time I helped Dorothy with a surgery."

Philip put down his mug of tea and took his hospital clothes to the laundry where he placed them with the other soiled clothes in the washing machine and then turned on the water and power. Then he went to see if there was anything Dorothy needed. He found her writing up her medical records, and she smiled at him. "He was in a bad way," she said, "I wonder what happened?"

"It was the Great White," replied Philip. Then he added, "You did a great job, honey."

"Thanks," Dorothy replied, "How could you tell? I mean, yes, what else could have done such damage, but did James say anything before he fainted?"

"No. But that damage to the cabin and cockpit, and the huge bite marks, are obviously the work of a Great White."

There was nothing that Dorothy needed him for, so Philip returned to where Andrea was sitting near James' bed. He carried in another chair and sat beside her. She turned to him and asked the same question.

"Philip? What do you suppose happened to James out there?"

"It was the shark. I saw the teeth marks on the cabin doorway and the cockpit coaming. That monster must have developed a taste for human flesh."

Andrea shuddered, and looked at James who still showed no signs of regaining consciousness. "What's going on, Philip?" she asked. "You know, *everything* was going so well for us until we reached these islands. Now it seems as though all the forces of hell have been unleashed against us. I mean, where is God in all of this?"

Philip was silent for a moment, looking at the floor. Then he said quietly, "Andrea, God has never moved His position. He gave us humans authority to rule over Planet Earth, and He gave us everything we needed to do that job! But our first parents, Adam and Eve, blew it. They disobeyed God's simple instructions, and He had warned them what would happen if they did. Since that far off day, our forefathers have continued to mess up. You and I have sinned...."

"But *how?*" Andrea broke in, "How did we sin? I was taught not to tell lies. I haven't hurt anyone, killed anyone, stolen anything."

"Andrea, tell me something," said Philip gently. "How is it that both you and James now feel that you should get married? It is because you *know* down on the inside that you should because it's the *right* thing to do, not so? This is your God-given conscience functioning. And I'm not talking about 'right' in terms of keeping society's rules. No, I'm talking about keeping God's law for right living.

"You knew deep down that living with James before getting married, was wrong, didn't you? Yet, you went ahead. Perhaps James told you it was okay?"

Andrea nodded, a miserable expression on her face. "So, are these sins so bad that God won't protect us from terrible danger?"

"If we deliberately live outside of God's laws, we come out from under His protection. God wants you to make a free-will decision to put your trust in His love for you, and to obey His ways, rather than trusting in your own ability to control your life, and to make up your own set of rules to live by. The Bible tells us that *all have sinned and fallen short of God's glory.* It also informs us that *the wages of sin is death.* There are consequences to sin."

"But Philip, I've always thought that I *was, I am,* a Christian. I mean, I was born in Canada, right? Isn't Canada a Christian nation?"

"Oh Andrea!" exclaimed Philip, and he sighed. "Canada is for the most part, *a godless nation!* So is the United States, and Great Britain. Did you know that statistics reveal that in the US, for example, there are, at most, fifty to sixty million Christians, out of a total population of more than two hundred and sixty million. That's less than one in four. I'm told that in Canada, the proportion is even less. I read somewhere, quite recently, that in the UK less than four percent of the population attend church. Are these Christian nations?"

"But, if God loves us, as you say, why doesn't He protect us?

Why does He allow suffering? There is so much suffering and misery in the world."

"You know Andrea, you are asking the correct questions, and they are tough questions. I believe there are good answers, but I'm not sure that you will understand them at present. But let me put it like this. God gave us authority to rule the earth; we disobeyed God, and we handed the authority over to Satan, who opposes God, and wants to kill, steal and destroy everything, because that is his evil nature. Humans are *not* in control of things, Satan is! In the apostle John's first letter, we read that *the whole world lies in the power of the evil one!* God's hands are tied, in a manner of speaking. Of course He could obliterate Satan, and start over. But God is perfect. He is perfect justice, for example. Even in the spiritual realms, He is perfect justice. So He cannot simply eliminate Satan, that would be pulling rank, bullying. God set up the rules, and He has to abide by them like everyone else. God has, and will overcome and punish Satan, but He will do it legally, in the High Courts of Heaven.

"God intended for humans to walk and talk with Him, to have a relationship with Him, and for us to manage this planet and keep Satan out of things. He gave us the authority and the means to do so. But Adam and Eve blew it. And every human being that has ever lived, except one, has continued to blow it! That is why the world is in such a mess. That is why there is so much suffering. *We are to blame, not God!"*

Andrea was following closely and she interrupted again. "Philip, if we are to blame, what's the solution? I mean, how can we escape from terrible danger and disasters? How can we get God to protect us?"

Philip turned to face the beautiful young woman sitting near by. "Oh, Andrea," he said, "That is what the gospel is all about! 'Gospel' means good news from God. He sent his very own Son, Jesus, the Christ, really part of Himself, to deal with the human sin problem.

Christ paid the penalty for sin, and when we put our trust in what He did, rather than in anything we try to do, He reconciles to God the Father. God gives us the peace and the inner strength to cope with dangers and disasters, rather than simply escape from them in this fallen world."

"I think I'm beginning to get it, to understand," said Andrea.

"Now, there is one more thing I must explain to you— *'Lord, open her eyes and her heart to understand this'*—I believe that both you and James have started searching for God. I believe that you are both 'seekers.'"

Philip saw Andrea nodding in agreement, and he continued. "Dorothy and I have been praying for you both. Perhaps there are others who are praying for you..."

"Yes, there are!" broke in Andrea, "James' mother, and his sister, Ruth. I know they are both praying for James and me."

"Well, this is the one other thing that I must explain to you, today. There is so much more to tell you, but the rest can wait. But this one thing... Look, the Bible informs us that there are only two camps, God's or Satan's. Everyone starts out in Satan's kingdom, by default. Then, when a person starts looking for truth, starts seeking God, Satan resists with all his might. Now, when someone prays for a person who is seeking truth, it is not unusual for the person being prayed for to come under fierce temptations or attacks of various kinds. This is because the powers of darkness do everything they can to hinder the person from discovering God's love. Actually, when a person does accept what Christ has done, Satan still does not let up. But, the devil can be resisted, and other Christians can help by nurturing, by supporting, the new convert."

At this point Philip could see that Andrea was struggling with something. "Have I confused you?" he asked her.

"No, not really," she flashed a smile at him. "But you speak as though Satan and the kingdom of darkness are so real, and that their sole purpose is to make our lives miserable."

"Oh, Andrea," Philip said quietly, "*You've said it*! When you become a Christian, you become a part of God's army against Satan. A Christian *is spiritual warfare!* This warfare is not an option. It is not something you may, or may not, want to engage in. No, you *are* in spiritual warfare, whether you like it or not. Satan hates God. Satan tried to pull off a coup and take over Heaven, long before humans came on the scene. But he only persuaded one third of the angels to join him, and they lost the battle and were thrown out of Heaven and cast down to the earth. He is a spirit-being, so we can't see him. But he's here, that's for sure. He lives in the *heavenly places;* that's the spiritual space around planet earth, or wherever humans are, even if they travel to outer space! These heavenly places are where he set up his kingdom of darkness, in opposition to God's purposes for humans.

"It's making so much sense to me," said Andrea, but Philip touched her arm.

"James is coming around," he said quietly, "We will need to watch him carefully, now. Many people are disoriented after anaesthetic, and can throw themselves around, fall out of bed, and so on."

It turned out that James was no exception. His eyes opened, and immediately he raised both hands as though trying to fend off some foe or other. Then he tried to get up, and Philip and Andrea had to use considerable force to restrain him. After a few minutes of struggling, he realized who they were, and slumped back on the bed. He was breathing hard from the exertion, and finally spoke, "Where am I? What has happened?"

Andrea climbed up on the bed, on the side of his good leg, and put her arms around him. "Darling," she said, "It's me. You are with me! You were attacked by the Great White shark, but you made it home to the island. You were badly injured, but Dorothy has operated on your leg, that's why you must keep still."

James had started to shake as the vivid memory of his ordeal came back into his mind. Andrea held him and rocked him very gently until his trembling stopped. "You've been through the mill, honey," she said. "But you made it! And everything is going to turn out well, now."

Philip came close and said to him, "James, you relax here. One of us will stay with you all the time. I'm going to go down to the dock and I will check that your boat is secure, so don't worry about the Robson. Then, I am going to bring some lunch, a very late lunch, for all of us."

After he had gone, Andrea kissed James again and again. "Oh my darling," she whispered, "I love you! Things are going to be okay. I've got so much to tell you. But you must rest now. I will be here, right here."

James felt sleep coming on, and he closed his eyes. Andrea climbed off the bed, and gently lowered his head onto the pillow once more. He was asleep when Philip returned with the lunch.

"I suspected he would be," he told Andrea. "Normally, one does not feel like eating after an operation. It's the drugs. But I've put the kettle on again for tea, and Dorothy will join us. I suggest," he went on, "than we take our chairs out this door, and we can eat and chat there without disturbing James."

When they had finished lunch, and were busy sipping tea, Andrea turned to Philip. "Is there any way that we could get a message to James' family? He had intended to call them from Cooktown in northern Queensland, but it doesn't look like we'll be there any time soon. I would also like to contact my parents."

"Yes, dear," said Philip. "There is a way. We keep a radio transmitter here in the clinic, in case of a medical emergency, and Dorothy needs special assistance. I also contact the Coast Guard in Ponape once every two weeks just to tell them we are fine. They asked me to, when we first made arrangements to live on this island."

16

After he had finished his tea, Philip led Andrea into Dorothy's little office and she saw the radio. Philip switched on the power, and once the set had warmed up, he tuned in to the Coast Guard at Ponape. After exchanging pleasantries for a few minutes, Philip told the operator about the three attacks made by the Great White shark. They discussed this at some length, and the operator said that he thought the captain at the base would probably want to talk further with Philip about it.

Then, Philip mentioned Andrea's request for a message to be relayed through to two sets of parents in Victoria. The man was very cooperative. "Doesn't she want to speak with them directly?" he asked. Andrea immediately nodded, and Philip relayed her answer.

"Well," the man drawled, "I'll fix that for her. Let me have their telephone numbers, and jest gimme a few minutes, say, ten minutes to arrange all the different connections, and I'll call you back."

It was forty minutes before he did call back. "It is ten at night, *yesterday*, in Victoria," he said by way of explanation. "But you're all set to start talkin."

Andrea could hear her mother on the other end, but at the same time there were other voices. "Hi everyone!" she said, and waited. A few seconds later she heard, first her Mom, then her Dad, then

James' mother and father, and finally, Ruth all greet her. They seemed to Andrea to all be in the same place, and using a speaker phone of some sort. She spoke again, "I've got some good and some bad news to tell you. We had an excellent sail from Hawaii, but were attacked by a Great White shark when we reached the Caroline Islands. Both James and I have written you letters, but these can only be mailed next week when a supply ship calls in at the island we are on...Truk Island, it's called. Anyway, James has a broken leg, and I have a broken arm..."

There was a babble of talk as every one the other end tried to ask questions at once. Then, Linda Barker came on clearly. "We all have lots of questions for you. But the main thing is, are you both all right?"

"Yes, Mom," said Andrea, "Tell my Mom and Dad, and tell Ruth, too, that we are fine, and both on the mend."

James' father came on next. "Lots of love to you both," he said, "How is the Robson?"

"A bit of a wreck," Andrea replied, "but nothing that can't be fixed."

Then her mother's voice came through. "Andy? Can you hear me? Andy, it's so good to hear your voice. We love you lots!"

Andrea smiled. 'Thanks Mom, Dad, everyone...love you all, too. Is Ruth there? Ruth, things are happening to us both...good things...I'll write again. Okay, the man says we should 'terminate'. So, love you all, Bye."

The radio operator's voice came through. "Are you there Philip? The captain wants to speak with you."

"Hi Jack," said Philip, "thanks very much for letting us do this...the young lady here, Andrea Jensen, thanks you, too. Okay, I'm ready for the skipper!"

Captain Brian Yuruchuk's voice came through. "Afternoon Philip. About the shark. You say it has attacked three times in about three or four days?"

Philip replied, "Yes Brian, three times in four days. We have a killer lurking out there, it has eaten five Islanders and they won't go out to fish anymore. I don't blame them. Is there anything you can do to help us?"

Yuruchuk answered immediately, "Yes, Philip. I will send the ship round to Truk tomorrow. It should reach you by 1400 hours. We have some equipment that might do the job. Did I hear you correctly? The shark has *killed and eaten five locals?"*

"Yes, Brian, it is a very serious situation that we have here. We need any help you can offer," replied Philip.

"I read you," said Yuruchuk, and he heard the radio connection click off.

In Victoria, British Columbia, five people enjoyed tea and fruit cake at the Barker's home where they had quickly assembled once they had been notified that the calls were coming through. They were excited to have heard Andrea's voice after several months' absence. The news was disturbing, and they talked about that, about sharks, and about the sea, but it was late, so the Jensens left about thirty five minutes after the radio conversation had ended. Ruth stayed on for a short while and she was excited. Linda Barker thought she knew why; she had caught the hint of an underlying message in Andrea's few words to her daughter.

Ruth's father had gone to bed, so she and her mother were alone. Ruth's eyes were shining, "Mom," she whispered, excitedly," did you hear what Andrea said? She said 'good things' had, or were, happening to both James and her."

"Yes, honey," replied her mother, "And I really believe that our prayers are being answered."

"Oh, I wish we could have spoken more freely, Mom. But it was great to hear their news, even the shark bit. I wonder how they both managed to break bones? I would have understood if they had said they received bites from the shark."

"Ruth," said her mother, "one does not just receive 'bites' from a Great White shark, as though the creature simply nibbles you! It can bite a person in two, and it can swallow a child whole! A Great White shark is a fearsome brute. To have broken Andrea' arm, and James' leg, must mean they had some sort of close encounter, but one in which the monster could not reach them to bite them."

"Oh," said Ruth, "well, anyway, the most important thing is that 'good things' are happening to them. Praise God! Okay, Mom, it's late, I must go."

17

Farulap had spent most of the day trying to reassure the fishermen in his village that God would protect them from the great man-eater out in the sea. But they were not convinced. He was becoming frustrated with them, but they simply pointed out, over and over, that God had not protected the five men who had been killed and eaten by the monster.

Most of the people in the village had listened to Philip when he had come early in the morning and spoken to them about the Sky God and His Son, Jesus. And most of those who had listened had marvelled at what Philip had told them. It was indeed, good news. To think that the Great God of the Heavens and the Earth, the Sky God Himself, had sent His Son to visit His creation.

They had been shocked to hear that cruel men had trapped the Sky God's Son, and had pierced Him through and through with strange little arrows until He had died. *Who would be so stupid as to do such a thing,* they asked one another? *Well, it was no wonder then, that things were continually going wrong for them. Things like storms, sickness, and of course, the killer shark's foul work.*

When Philip had told them that Jesus had risen up from his burial place three days after they had laid his body on the burial platform, a great rejoicing had broken out among them. They had all leapt to their feet and started singing and dancing. He had not been able to speak any more, because of their excitement, so he had gone back to his house after telling Farulap that he would tell them more another day when they called him.

Some of the fishermen told Farulap that God had protected him from the shark because he used to be the village holy man. But they said that God had not protected the other five victims because they were ordinary folk just as they themselves were. They told him that they believed that he had met the Sky God in a new and marvellous way, but they had not found this way yet, for themselves. In the end, they agreed that Farulap should get Philip to tell them more 'good news.'

Farulap had even said he was prepared to demonstrate to them all that the Sky God would protect him now, because he had become a member of the Sky God's own family. He would go fishing the next morning, and then they would understand what this good news was all about.

The fishermen had gone silent when Farulap had said this, and had held a quiet discussion among themselves. Then, they had agreed that it was a good idea. Perhaps the Sky God would not only protect Farulap from the shark, but He might give him such a large catch of fish that the whole village could have a 'party.' No one had eaten fresh fish for many days, and they were getting tired of the dried stuff they stored up for lean times. They would gather on the beach and watch to see what would happen.

Back in the little hospital room, James Barker stirred out of his sleep at six forty-five that evening, and saw Andrea sitting beside his bed. He looked around still a little disoriented, and then it all came back to him. He focussed his thoughts on his leg, *to feel it,* and became aware that the dull ache he had been conscious of, was, in fact, coming from his left leg. Andrea noticed that James was awake, and she put down the magazine she was reading. Taking one of his hands in her right hand, she leaned forward. "How are you feeling, honey?"

"A lot better," he replied.... "Have I told you what happened out there?"

"No," she replied, "You haven't had an opportunity up until now."

"Well..." he said, and before he could continue, Andrea interrupted him.

"Wait," she said quickly, "I know that Philip, and perhaps Dorothy, too, will want to hear what happened. I'll run and tell them you are awake."

All three were soon back in the hospital room, with Philip bringing in one more chair. They settled themselves, and Dorothy spoke first. "James, you sure were given the 'once over' by that shark! I was very impressed, after I saw your injuries, to realize that you made it back to the dock by yourself."

Philip nodded in agreement, and told James that the Coast Guard were sending a ship over the next day, to attempt to deal with the shark. "But, tell us," he said, "What happened to you out there?"

James leaned back on his pillows. "I had a wonderful sail for the first hour or so. I tested the backstay fitting, and it seemed fine when running down wind. The conditions were so perfect, that I just relaxed out there, at one with the boat, the sea, and the wind.

"Then, I leaned forward to swat a fly that had settled on my leg and a waterfall, literally speaking, hit me from behind. Just water. It knocked me halfway down into the cockpit well, and I guess that was the first thing that saved my life. Because, a second or two later, The Great White fell down on top of the cockpit! It must have jumped right out of the ocean onto the yacht. If I had been sitting normally on the seat, I would have been crushed to death."

"You had absolutely no prior warning?" asked Philip.

"Absolutely none whatsoever! I vaguely remember the sun being blocked out, like a huge shadow came over the boat, or at least over me. Then, I was squashed down into the cockpit well by the belly of the shark because it landed across and slightly on the port—er—left side. I think it must have been the shark's right pectoral fin that slammed me down onto the cockpit sole, onto the grid base that is there." Barker shuddered as he recalled the shattering events, and he was unable to talk for several minutes.

"If this is too much for you, you don't have to continue," said Dorothy.

"No, no," Barker replied, opening his eyes again, and leaning forward. "Okay, let me see... Yes, I remember a terrific pain in my left leg, low down, and then in my nose as I was slammed onto the grid." He shook his head as if the whole episode was just a nightmare. "My face was to one side, I think it was to the right, and suddenly I was under water. For a few seconds I thought the Robson had sunk, that we were going down. It was dark, too, under the shark like that." He shuddered again, and then continued.

"The yacht heeled over very sharply to port, and the water drained away. At that point I was able to get some air again. Then the boat seemed to rock wildly and I heard a very loud report, which I realize now was the mast breaking above. No backstay, again, and a following wind, plus violent movements caused by the Great White. I felt some very rough rubbing from that pectoral fin as the monster thrashed around. Then, suddenly it was gone."

"What did you do then?" It was Andrea who asked in a small voice. She was living through the whole episode with Barker as he was telling what happened. Dorothy and Philip could see that James' vivid description was bringing back to Andrea's memory her own traumatic encounter with the shark.

Barker lay back on his pillow again. "In a way, the aftermath was the worst part," he said. "I remember the terrible pain, tasting blood from my leg, or nose, I'm not certain which. And when I saw the bones sticking out of my leg, I nearly freaked! Then I remember thinking, 'I still have an engine.' *Isn't that amazing?* Yes, I still have an engine! So I got it started. Oh, and I also had to fasten a wrench onto the stub of the broken tiller so that I could steer the boat.

"On the way back to the dock, I felt myself fainting several times, and I forced myself to carry on..." his voice trailed off, and all four were silent for a long time. Finally, he spoke very softly. "I guess I'm lucky to be alive, hey?"

"No, James," said Philip quietly, "not lucky. *You were brought through!*"

Philip, Dorothy and Andrea took it in turns to stay up through the night with Barker. Their shifts were of three hours duration, but Dorothy suggested that Andrea sleep in the adjacent little room which had the second bed. With her wanting to be near James the whole night, this arrangement worked well. The main issue concerned his leg. He had to be watched continuously to ensure that he didn't move it and disturb the bones so delicately repositioned after being broken.

This meant considerable discomfort for Barker, who dearly wished he could change his position and turn over from time to time. But he was a good patient and cooperated, knowing that the others were going without sleep themselves, and all on his account. Dorothy had told him that if the swelling around the break had subsided a little by the morning, then she would apply the first of two or perhaps three casts that he would need until the bones were knitted together. The good news, then, was that once a cast was in place, he would be able to sleep and turn without disturbing things.

Andrea had the final shift of the night, from three until six a.m. Philip woke her when his shift was over, and as soon as he had left for the cottage, she climbed into James' bed and snuggled up beside him. He was awake, and in considerable pain, and was waiting for the drugs Philip had given him, to take effect. They lay close together and talked quietly for a while. Then Andrea realized that she kept falling asleep, and would not be doing her leg-watching duty if this happened. So she reluctantly sat in the chair and kept a close eye on James' movements.

Dorothy was a very welcome sight when she arrived with hot coffee and rusks shortly after six thirty. Neither Barker nor Andrea had tasted a rusk before, and learned from Dorothy that they were basically dried sweet bread that had been sliced into thick pieces. The Kitsons had discovered rusks on a trip to South Africa, and had recognized their practical value in being able to be stored for months or even years under airtight conditions.

They watched Dorothy dunk her rusk in the mug of hot coffee, and then bite off the piece that had softened. Soon they were dunking away, and wishing they had known about rusks before they set off on their voyage.

When the coffee and rusks had been consumed, Dorothy made a close inspection of Barker's leg. She decided that the first plaster cast could be applied, and enlisted Andrea's help. It was completed and setting within an hour, and Andrea went off to the cottage to shower. Barker lay back in the pillows on his bed, and fell asleep once more.

As the morning progressed, a new weather front approached the island. Heavy clouds settled over the Carolines, and the wind picked up in strength. This had the effect of kicking up moderate to large waves, and made it impossible for Farulap to embark on his fishing-in-faith demonstration. The Islanders understood the weather, and they all agreed that the demonstration proposed by Farulap could wait a day or two.

Philip Kitson was sitting in the lounge of the cottage when Andrea emerged from the spare bedroom. She was wearing a brightly coloured shorts and tee-shirt matching outfit, and her beauty took

Philip's breath away.

"Wow, Andrea!" he exclaimed, "You look stunning! You had better not walk in on James too suddenly, he might do something rash, and injure his leg again."

Andrea smiled impishly. "Glad you like it," she said, "I took this along with me in case we got marooned on a desert island!"

Kitson chuckled. *"Full many a flower is born to blush unseen,"* he said, *"and waste its fragrance on the desert air....,* or something like that."

"What are you reading?" she asked.

"Oh," he replied, looking down at his open Bible, "I am reading John, chapter one. An amazing piece of scripture, of course all scripture has its messages, but this piece has always been a favourite of mine."

"Do you read your Bible every day?" she asked.

"No," he said, "not every day. But I would like to. Sometimes other things crop up, and I get busy. However, I don't sweat about it, I just read it whenever I can."

Andrea sat down on the sofa opposite him, and said, "Philip, would you show me how *you* read your Bible? You know, I tried once, but I couldn't seem to get the hang of it, and I lost interest. Would you mind, I mean, just for a minute?"

"I would be delighted, my dear," he said. "Listen to this:

In the beginning was the Word, and the Word was with God, and the Word was God. He was in the beginning with God. All things came into being by Him; and apart from Him nothing came into being that has come into being. In Him was life, and the life was the light of men."

"That is from chapter one, verses one to three."

"I know that I have heard that before, sometime," said Andrea, "but what exactly does it mean?"

"Let me tell you how I see it," Philip replied. "Firstly, it says, *In* *the beginning...*Now, that gives us a number of things to think about. The first sentence in the first chapter of the first book in the Bible, that's the book called Genesis, says, *In the beginning God...* So, I see a connection, do you?"

Andrea nodded.

"Well," he continued, "the connection that I see is this: the Word that was *in the beginning*, must have been connected to God, the same God we read about in Genesis. Actually, it goes on in John 1, verse 1, to say exactly that. The Word *is* God. Then, in the next verse it turns from the impersonal to the personal sense: *He*—that is, the Word—*was in the beginning with God.* So now we discover something else. There is God, the eternal, self-sufficient, all powerful, and all knowing, Supreme Being. But there is another Being who is with God, who is called *the Word.*

"So, Jesus Christ is the expression of God to human beings. Later on in the chapter, in verses fourteen and eighteen, John says this plainly. This means that Christ is one with God, yet is distinct, too. Verse three tells us that Christ is the Creator, He made everything there is.

"Now, I wanted to check that out. I wanted to see if it said *Christ is the Creator* anywhere else in the scriptures. So, I looked at the cross references—here, let me show you what I mean—and I found Colossians 1:15 to 17, and also Hebrews 1: 1-3. Do you see those? I looked them up and they all say exactly the same thing!

"So, you see Andrea, I just read a few verses of the Bible, and I consider them carefully. Actually, I use a little formula: 'what does it really say; what does it mean; is there something God is saying to me, personally? That's how I read my Bible."

"*That is fascinating*," said Andrea. "Oh, Philip, I would love it if you would teach me more from the Bible. Do you think you could?"

"Sure," he replied, "Do you think James might be interested, too?"

"I think so!" she said, "And what else can he do, but listen," and she winked at Philip.

18

Would you come down to the boat with me," asked Andrea. "I know James will be worrying about it, whether it is securely moored at the dock."

Philip smiled. "It's okay," he said. "I went down early this morning and tied the lines at the front and the back of the boat. But let's go down anyway, and together we might be able to sort out the mess of sails and cables. I could not do those on my own. First, though, let's swing by the clinic and see how James is doing."

James was sleeping, and able to change position now that the cast was on his leg. He was making up for his relatively uncomfortable and sleepless night. Five minutes later, Philip and Andrea climbed on board the Robson. The damage caused by the shark was terrible to see. Andrea was glad that James was not with them, and she hoped that she might be able to do some repairs herself, before he was able to move about.

With Andrea assisting with one arm, Philip was able to remove the main-sail from the boom, and then pull it down the slot in the broken mast. Together they began to unravel one tangle of shroud and stay cables, and Philip rolled this neatly into a separate coil. He asked Andrea whether it would be useful to tag each one for easy identification later. But she smiled and pointed out that the turnbuckles were either red for the port side, or green for those that were on the starboard side. James, she told Philip, was meticulous about those kinds of things. Then they continued, tidying up the mess item by item.

One hundred miles to the east of Truk Island, the United States Coast Guard ship USCG 401, was moving at a steady twenty two knots. Her sharp bow was slicing through the moderate chop and the powerful engines left a creamy wake behind. Captain Brian Yuruchuk was on the bridge with one eye on the sea ahead, and the other on the drawing his second mate was trying to explain to him.

"Skipper," said the second mate, "I'm confident that this will work."

Yuruchuk was not so sure. "Jimmy," he said, "Do you have any idea what sort of monster we are dealing with? Do you realize that the Great White shark, *Carcharodon carcharias* by name, could be twenty five feet long, and weigh in at several tons? This one, that has killed and eaten God-knows how many people, might even be twenty percent bigger all round."

"Skipper, I've bounced my plan off Dobson, he claims he knows all about sharks, and especially Great Whites. He reckons this idea might be just the perfect thing to rid us of this brute."

Yuruchuk rolled his eyes, and snorted. "*Dobson,*" he said, "did Dobson volunteer to go with you in the life boat?"

"Yes sir!" said Jimmy Bartholomew, the second mate. "I have no shortage of volunteers for this task. There's Dobson, Carvalho, Jennings, Hickson, Williamson..."

"Yeah, yeah, I know," sighed Yuruchuk. "You guys just want the adventure. Bored hey? Well, it has been kinda quiet, these last few months. Okay. I tell you what. When we are another fifty miles closer to our destination, that will be in two hours, I will stop the ship and you will do a practice run, okay? I want you to do a demonstration for me. Go and tell your crew, your 'volunteers', to get ready, to get *everything* ready. I'll give you forty five minutes, then we move on. I said we would be off Truk at 1400 hours."

Bartholomew informed his volunteers of the captain's instructions. "He wants us to do a test run," the second mate told them. "Let's get everything ready to go."

'Everything' included machetes for each man, the harpoon gun with four projectiles, and copious lengths of braided rope. What Bartholomew did not disclose, even to his crew, was the single depth charge he had hidden in the stern locker of the life boat. This would be within easy reach of his position at the helm, and was there 'just in case'. The second mate could not have articulated what the 'just in case' might be, but he felt more comfortable with the explosive in the locker.

The life boat was ready to go in twenty minutes, and Bartholomew wondered how many people could have drowned during that time, had there been an emergency. However he knew that his crew were not regulars on this end of things, being comprised mainly of cooks and assistant mechanics who served most of their time in the kitchen or the engine room. These men were his personal buddies, and he knew that the captain knew that, too.

Yuruchuk was a good guy, thought Bartholomew. He was easy going, but strict when he had to be. The men respected their skipper, and knew that he was a careful leader. This test run, or demonstration, as the skipper called it, was just another illustration of the thoroughness with which they carried out their duties under his command.

Exactly two hours after the skipper had spoken, he brought the ship to a stop. There was a fairly strong wind blowing, but the sea was calm in the lee of Oroluk Island. Bartholomew and his men were ready, and the life boat was lowered fairly quickly. They had a large white plastic pontoon with them, the kind the crew often used on exercises at sea. This, the second mate had informed Captain Yuruchuk, was a dummy Great White shark.

With most of the ship's crew gathered at the port rails, to watch the 'shark killers' in action, Bartholomew and his men went about their test run. This involved dumping the pontoon overboard, and then retreating a few hundred yards away. At the second mate's signal, the life boat speeded around the sea as though pursuing some hidden enemy that was fleeing away—or they were trying to escape if perhaps the enemy was chasing them—the skipper was not sure which. But he got the picture, and when the Portuguese, Carvalho, fired the harpoon and made a direct hit, a mighty cheer went up from the ship's crew. Using the ships loud hailer, Yuruchuk congratulated Bartholomew and his men, and told them to come back on board the ship without delay. Fifteen minutes later, they were increasing speed towards Truk Island.

With the broken mast removed and lying on the dock, with the sails dried and folded neatly into their bags, and with all the tangle of shroud and stay cables rolled and stowed away in the cockpit locker, *Skipping Stone* had begun to look more like a boat and less like a wreck. Andrea had washed down the decks and the cockpit, removing the blood stains and cleaning the topsides. The cabin hatch had been destroyed by the shark, but James, who had anticipated a hatch being damaged by a rogue wave, had a spare behind the engine. Andrea remembered this, recalling the surprise James' father had expressed when he had seen James stowing it away.

The grooves down which the hatch was designed to slide, had been badly damaged by the shark, but there was enough left to get the hatch closed against any rainfall. Andrea was pleased with the clean up job, and she joined Philip on the dock to look things over from a distance. She heard Philip chuckling, and looked at him inquiringly.

"I was just thinking how much better *Skipping Stone* looks now, compared to when we arrived down here an hour and a half ago, he said. "Back then, I was recalling what a university chum used to say when I parked my battered little car next to his smart new pickup. He would say, 'Who's had an accident and left the wreckage here?'"

Andrea smiled, but he could see that there was also sadness in her eyes as she surveyed what had been until recently, a very smart sail boat, and a comfortable home for James and herself. Philip took her arm and said, "Andrea, remember how James fixed that gaping hole in the stern? Most of the damage we see can be fixed in the same way. There are some things that will need to be repaired in a boatyard, but James will get that under way when he recovers. In the meantime, Dorothy and I are so enjoying your company, despite the medical problems, and we would like for you two to stay for as long as you wish."

She smiled up at him, and he continued. "Now, we should check on James again, and see if he is awake. The Coast Guard will be coming in about forty minutes, and the captain will probably want to interview both James and you. They are hoping to catch or frighten off the shark so that the Islanders can start fishing again."

James was awake, so Andrea fixed some lunch and sat eating it with him in his room. She waited until he asked about the Robson, and then she told him what she and Philip had done. He was especially pleased that she had put the spare hatch in place.

At five minutes to two, USCG 401 arrived and dropped anchor off the reef. In minutes, a highly powered inflatable was speeding through the lagoon and up to the dock. Captain Yuruchuk and his second mate, Jimmy Bartholomew, stepped ashore. The ship was left in the capable hands of the first mate, who was just a little peeved that Bartholomew had seen so much action in one day.

They were met by Philip Kitson, who led the way to the clinic. Dorothy joined them and they filed in to meet James and Andrea.

Both visitors were awestruck at the beautiful young woman who sat at Barker's bedside. But they recovered their composure and began the interview, with Yuruchuk asking most of the questions, and Bartholomew taking notes. Then they outlined the strategy they thought of trying out on the shark.

It was James who commented first. "I sure hope it works," he said, "because that is one *mean critter*. It may try to jump onto your lifeboat, so beware."

Andrea thought of something, and turned to Yuruchuk. "Captain," she said, "Would it be possible for you to mail some letters in Ponape? We have written to our folks back home, and we have been waiting for the supply ship."

"I'd be delighted to help you," Yuruchuk replied. "We will be back before the supply ship, if all goes well here. In fact," he said, "If you wish to write more letters while we are busy trying to deal with the shark, we can pick them up before we sail."

She hurried back to the cottage, and gathered up their writing materials and the letters previously written. On her return to the clinic, she met Yuruchuk and Bartholomew who were about to leave. She handed the letters to the captain, and said she would like to write others. He put them in a small brief case he had with him, and was heading back to the ship within a few minutes.

Back at USCG 401, Bartholomew's crew had lowered the lifeboat loaded with their gear, and were waiting for him to return. As he climbed out of the inflatable to board the ship's ladder, Yuruchuk gave them the 'go ahead'. "Use your intercom if you need help," he said, and they motored out in the direction of Hall Island.

For three hours the lifeboat and the adventurous seamen cruised the waters that Philip Kitson had pointed out as the location of two of the shark attacks. But there was no sign of the great white. Disappointed, they returned to the ship, refuelled, and secured the lifeboat against the side boarding platform. They decided it would be best to try again in the morning.

Andrea sat with James, and they both were writing letters. Philip had walked off to see how Farulap and some of the recent converts to Christ, were progressing. Dorothy was busy teaching several local women basic hygiene and child care. She recalled that when they had first arrived, infant mortality on Truk had been alarmingly high. The Islanders seemed resigned to it, and told Philip that it was because of the displeasure of the gods that their babies died.

But Dorothy had known better. She had seen the unsanitary conditions the people lived under, and the polluted water they were drinking. She saw the lack of personal hygiene, and the carelessness with food preparation. She knew that the unholy gods, the devil and his demons, were very pleased at the suffering! So she went to work, treating the dysentery, wounds, and other diseases, while Philip worked with the men. He had tackled the drinking water supplies first. When the men showed him the village watering hole, a dirty little pothole in a stream which flowed down from the forest above their village, he was appalled. Going only fifty yards higher up the stream, he had found a spot where he could construct a small weir. Two men helped him, while several others stood and watched in fascination.

In less than a day, he had dammed the creek and the sediment in the water began to settle out leaving much cleaner water flowing down stream. However, Philip knew this was not the total solution to the problem.

He ordered a one hundred yard roll of plastic piping, one inch diameter, and when the monthly supply ship delivered it, Philip piped clean water from the little dam down to a mound of stones he had placed immediately above the pothole. From a stainless steel pipe set into the mound of stones, a crystal-clear stream dropped two feet into the pothole enabling the women to fill their containers with uncontaminated water. Almost immediately, with improved hygiene, cooking, and clean drinking water, infant mortality dropped to a virtual zero. Fewer sick people showed up at the clinic, and Dorothy was delighted with the results.

The next project Philip and Dorothy had turned their attention to, was the sewage disposal problem. The Islanders simply defecated anywhere, some even outside their little homes. The flies were numerous, and the stench was bad, especially on a windless day. Dorothy had spoken to the women about it, and they showed some interest in the issue, but both Philip and Dorothy had realized that something practical, and convenient, would be required if they were to succeed in dealing successfully with this matter.

Philip had a brainwave one day. He had prayed long and hard, asking for divine wisdom. One morning when he had walked up to the village, a plan had begun to materialize in his mind. If he could get the men to help him dig a narrow, but deep trench, about forty yards long, and down wind of the village, he thought to himself, perhaps he could persuade them to defecate into this trench. Then, at least once a week, but preferably daily, someone could dump a little soil onto the excrement to cover it.... Perhaps he could even train them to understand the importance of covering with soil immediately...and perhaps they would progress to washing their hands afterwards...

At first, the Island people had not been as enthusiastic over his idea as he had wished. But again, he had found the two willing helpers, and they spent a week digging the trench, and putting up a short bamboo screen to separate it from the nearest dwellings in the village. Then, one morning he called for a gathering of all the people, telling them that he and the 'doctor' would show them pictures.

Calling the people to order by clapping his hands, Philip had then dropped his first bombshell. He waved his Bible at them and with his incomplete grasp of their language at the time, had managed to get his message across: *I have shown you this book with the Sky God's words. Now He has told us how to live lives free from sickness. And the Sky God has told us how to deal with our body wastes. It is all in here!*

Then, with several medical journals and text books he and Dorothy had brought along to the meeting, they showed the villagers some of the coloured pictures of gross deformities and other horrible effects of disease on human bodies. The people, who were always fascinated by books and pictures, spent hours poring over these books, chattering loudly to each other. Eventually, Philip delivered his second bombshell: *If they did not want to end up with similar horrible sicknesses, then they should change the way they handled their sewage.*

After further discussion among themselves, Philip had understood that the people's consensus was to cooperate! He then managed to convey to them, that a work party was required to collect all the excrement lying around the village, and dump it into the trench. Amazingly, the people had no problem with this, and in a matter of hours, the place had been cleaned up.

Finally, he had led them all behind the screen, and personally covered the mess in the trench with a thin layer of the soil dumped behind the trench. Then he invited Dorothy to come and see. With a display of great approval, Dorothy made it very clear that this was the right thing to do.

Philip had next invited the villagers to 'come and see.' There was a great deal of chattering, and gestures of acceptance, as though they themselves had thought up the whole idea. Over the course of the following months, apart from occasional slip-ups, the people used the screened off trench and another problem was solved.

19

The morning after the USCG 401's arrival dawned bright and clear. It was one of those perfect days that the islands of the Pacific Ocean are famous for. Not a cloud in the sky, and just a whisper of a breeze which hardly rippled the surface of the sea.

In the Islanders' village, Farulap had woken early, and together with a dozen men, had made his way to the beach near the dock. He was all set for his demonstration of fishing-in-faith, quite confident that now he was a Christian, God would protect him from the Great White shark.

The other fishermen watched him climb into a borrowed catamaran, complete with fishing tackle, and raise the rattan sail. With help from his paddle, he was soon clear of the reef bordering the lagoon, and heading for the favourite fishing spot—the spot where five men had lost their lives only a few days previously. Quite soon he was a small figure on the horizon, and the men sat down on the beach and waited.

Philip was up early, as usual, and emerging from his shower, he dressed and walked into the lounge to spend a few minutes reading his Bible. But first, he looked out at the ship, and noticed how clear and bright the sky was. About to turn away, his eyes caught sight of a catamaran with a lone occupant heading for the reef. He was alarmed. Who was it? Then, looking down to the beach, he saw the waiting men.

Philip hurried out and down to the beach. From these fishermen, he learned about Farulap's venture of faith. Hurrying back to the cottage, he switched on the power to his radio, and tuned in to the ship's frequency. The ship's radio operator sounded cheerful.

"Good morning to you," replied Kitson into his microphone. "This is Philip Kitson on Truk Island. Is the captain up at this hour?"

Almost immediately, Yuruchuk's voice came through. "Hi, Philip. What's up?"

"There may be a complication to your work this morning, Brian. One of the fishermen here, has gone out to the reef where there was an attack a couple of days ago. He is alone, and may be ripe pickings for the shark."

"Yes Philip, the watch reported him to me a short while ago. But I've been thinking, going over the reports of the attacks, and something has come to mind. Let me bounce it off you. All the attacks by the Great White occurred to sailing or stationary vessels. *None took place when an engine was driving a vessel, right?"*

"Correct," answered Kitson, "Do you think an engine is a deterrent, that the shark only goes for silent vessels?"

"I am wondering about that. Anyway, I have a plan. We could rig the lifeboat to sail, it has the equipment on board. It is a simple sprit rig that can be stowed in the long locker on the one side of the boat. I think we will motor across to where the fisherman has gone, and then cut the engine. The crew will raise the boat's sailing rig, and cruise around silently in that vicinity. What do you think of that?"

"It sounds well worth trying, Brian, my only concern is for the fisherman, though. What if the shark attacks him?"

"Well, I can't do much about that, I'm afraid. The guy has gone out there voluntarily. But, what we aim to do, is be right near him, and ready for the shark if it makes an appearance."

Kitson heard no more from Yuruchuk. He was watching from the lounge window when Andrea came in, and joined him there.

"What an exquisite day!" she exclaimed.

"Yes," he replied. "But there could be some excitement this morning." Then he told her what Farulap was doing, and the Coast Guard's plan for the morning.

"I'm going to take some breakfast up to James, and I'll tell him what's afoot," she said.

When Andrea had given James his breakfast, she informed him of the goings on out near the reef. He shook his head. "None of them out there seem to realize what this shark does. He doesn't simply surface and swim around saying, 'Okay guys, am I nicely positioned for a harpoon shot now?' He leaps out of the water without the slightest warning, and crashes down on your boat."

Andrea understood this only too well. "What can we do," she asked him.

"I doubt that there is anything we could do," he replied.

"We could pray," she said tentatively, watching James' face.

But he cast a strange glance in her direction, and muttered, "I don't believe God is into that kind of stuff..." Then, more loudly, "No. I'm not sure that God pays attention to an individual's problems. I think if He listens at all, it must only be to things of national, or perhaps city-wide importance...Anyway, I'm not sure about God, at all."

Andrea was silent for a long moment. "James, she said, "I have seen Philip reading his Bible nearly every day. So, I asked him about it, you know, how to read it, how to make sense of it all. And he showed me. It was wonderful! It was as though the drapes were pulled back from the windows of my mind. I saw so many wonderful things, in just a few verses...And I asked him if he would teach me more things in the Bible."

It was James' turn to be silent for a long while. Then he said,

"Andrea, my sweet, I have so many problems with the Bible. I mean, the first chapter is clearly wrong about creation. Maybe there's parts of the Bible that have a lesson for us to learn, but how do we pick and choose?"

"Philip said he would be happy to teach you and me, together, if we wanted him to. What do you think? You know, you are just lying here, you can't move around, and you shouldn't, anyway. Would you be willing?"

"Well, I don't know," he said, "I don't want to start arguing with him about creation and stuff. Philip is such a wonderful guy." James looked at Andrea and saw disappointment in her face, and relented. "Well, okay. I will just keep silent when I know he's 'out to lunch' with some of the things he tells us. Sure, let's do it."

She moved over to the bed, leaned down and kissed him lingeringly on the mouth. Suddenly he pulled back. "Whoa, honey!" he gasped, "You can't just do that sort of thing to me when I am in this condition, helpless 'an all'! You just wait 'til I am well!"

"You mean, until we are married?" she said mischievously, and he grinned.

"Hey, honey! How about Philip marrying us today, then?"

"Ima gonna see what is happenin' with that there shark hunt," she drawled in reply, pretending she hadn't heard, and smiled at him as she left.

A great deal had happened out on the water near the reef. Firstly, Farulap had baited up his hooks and dropped several lines over the side of the catamaran's starboard hull. Almost immediately, he was catching fish. It seemed to him that they were hungrier than ever before, and he took this as a sign of God's pleasure with his act of faith. Quite soon, he had so many fish that he moved over to the other hull and began to fill that one up as well.

He had been there only about half an hour, when he saw the lifeboat with her armed crew, approaching. To his astonishment, he heard them stop their engine, and start to put up a little sail. This seemed to take them a very long time, and once the boat was rigged, they sailed it around and around, quite near him. He wondered if this was some sort of religious ritual, or perhaps that they were hoping for fish to float to the surface, or some other miracle to take place. But nothing he could see, happened.

Two hours later, Farulap decided that God had honoured his step of faith. His catamaran was full of fish, so he pulled up his lines and paddled over to the lifeboat. He was feeling sorry for these people, whose strange behaviour had not netted them any fish. Bartholomew saw him coming, and loosened the sheet to spill wind from the spritsail. When Farulap came along side, he held up a large rockfish and offered it to them. Bartholomew was both surprised and delighted, and with many gestures conveyed his appreciation. Then shaking their heads, the crew watched him adjust his sail and head off to Truk Island.

"I don't know about you, boys," said the second mate, "But I have a feeling that shark has left this area, and so should we!"

With that, he turned the ship around, ordered the sail to be taken down and the rig stored, and he motored back to the ship. When they arrived at the boarding platform, he left the crew with the chore of securing the lifeboat while he took the fish up to the kitchen.

Yuruchuk had watched him coming up the ladder, and was in the galley waiting for him. "Well done, Second Mate!" he said cheerfully. "Thank you for your gift of appreciation to me and the First Mate for letting you have so much fun these last two days." Taking the fish out of the astonished second mate's hands, he gave it to the cook. "You know how we both like our fresh fish done now, don't you, chef?"

Then the skipper turned back to Bartholomew, whose mouth was still open in surprise. "Well," he said, "Don't just stand there gaping at me, man. There's a Great White shark to be caught. Come on, get to it!"

The second mate recovered. "Sir," he said. "Why is it that I think there is something wrong with this picture? No, but seriously Skipper, sir, I have a feeling that shark has long gone. It's not around these parts anymore."

"That may be so, Second Mate," replied the captain, "But we have to be sure. It would not look right if we up and left after such a short search. Keep at it and come back at seventeen hundred hours."

When Farulap reached the beach, almost everyone from the village was there to meet him. And, when they saw the great bounty of fish in the two hulls of the catamaran, he was applauded. But he called them to attention, and spoke to them as they gathered around him. Philip had seen him coming in to the lagoon, and had gone down to hear what he had seen and done out at the reef. Later that evening, Philip told Dorothy, Andrea, and James as they sat in the little hospital room, having their supper together.

"So, Farulap called all the throng of people to attention," he said. "And this is what he told them. 'People: The Sky God protected me today. He told me in my spirit,'—Farulap pointed to his stomach, at that point—'that He was pleased with my trust in Him. And so He rewarded me, and all of you, by giving me this great catch of fish that you see here. I have shown you that we no longer have to fear the monster fish, and we can return to the reef and catch fish just as our fathers did. Now, I want us to pay homage to the Sky God!'"

"He then fell down flat on his face on the sand, and so did everyone else!" continued Philip. "It was quite amazing. They all began to praise God at once, and they kept it up for quite a while."

"Did you speak to him at all?" asked Dorothy.

"No," said Philip, "I felt that it was God's moment, and it was Farulap's moment. So I came away quietly."

Later that evening, Captain Brian Yuruchuk contacted Philip

Kitson by radio, and said that his men had seen no sign of the shark. They were convinced, he said, that it had moved elsewhere, and he agreed with them. The base had called him and he needed to attend to other matters fairly urgently. His ship would leave at O800 the following morning, but before that, he could send an inflatable to the dock at 0715, to collect any additional letters for mailing in Ponape. Kitson thanked him for his kindness, and the conversation ended.

It had been an eventful day, and they were all feeling weary. James' leg pain had subsided considerably, and he was feeling much better. When the others retired to bed, he lay awake for a long time. His thoughts returned to the conversation that Andrea had with him that morning. He could see that she was keen to learn more about the Bible, and he did not wish to discourage her in any way. But, as far as he was concerned, he would just tag along. *After all,* he thought, *what harm could it do?*

20

Andrea slept in the cottage that night, and she arrived back at the little hospital room at seven the next morning with a tray carrying hot porridge, milk, and brown sugar. There were two slices of toast and strawberry jam. In a flask, coffee was being kept hot.

"Hi honey," she said, and James returned her greeting. After she had put the tray down on the bedside table, he pulled her down onto his lap and they smooched for a while. Then she stood up and put her hands on her hips. "Well, Mr Barker," she said, "Are you going to eat me or your breakfast?"

Barker grinned. "Both should do me fine, but the porridge is getting cold."

They finished their breakfast and were about to pour the coffee when Philip walked in carrying three Bibles and his own mug of tea. "How are you feeling, James?" he asked.

"Pretty good," replied Barker. "I see you have come to *edumakate* us," and he chuckled.

"Well, yes," said Philip, "the *system* doesn't do a very good job on us these days. So, I'm here at your disposal. Please feel free to decline, or applaud, or ask any questions you like. The ones I can't answer, I will refer to Dorothy!"

He sipped his tea. Then he said seriously, "Andrea asked if I would teach both of you some of my favourite parts of the Bible. So, I'm ready. I've brought along a Bible for each of you, in case you want to follow, and read for yourselves. Okay? Are you happy for me to do this today, or would you prefer to wait for another occasion?"

"Oh no, I mean yes! I would love you to start today," enthused Andrea and she looked at James. He shrugged, "Sure, Philip, today feels okay with me."

"Good," said Philip, "Now, I am going to suggest that we start at the very beginning, in Genesis chapter one. Let's open our Bibles to that spot. Genesis is properly described as the book of beginnings, and it gets right at it. Would you like to read that first verse, Andrea?"

She found the place and read: *'In the beginning God created the heavens and the earth.'* Then she looked up.

Philip kept his finger on the page and said, "Now, let's pause here and consider several things. First, it states quite clearly that there *was* a beginning, a start to things, but that God was already there. What does that mean? It means that at one point, time did not exist. Neither did matter, nor energy, nor space as we know those dimensions. It means that there did come a moment when God initiated energy, matter, space and time. Before that, only God, and another dimension, a *spiritual dimension,* existed.

"Is this okay so far," he asked, and both James and Andrea nodded. Continuing, he said, "Next, we need to consider the word translated as 'God'. The original Hebrew word is *Elohim,* which means 'the uni-plural Supreme Being.' It is an unusual word, having plural capacity, yet definitely emphasising that God is One. It also carries the meaning of 'Creator' and especially, 'One who created us for His own pleasure.'

"Now, in the beginning, *Elohim,* the uni-plural God, decided to create a physical universe. Who is this Creator God?

"Jesus of Nazareth claimed directly and indirectly on many

occasions to be God in human flesh-and rose from the dead to prove it! He is described in three New Testament passages of scripture as the Creator of all things visible and invisible, and that His power holds all things together. Let's take a look at those verses in our Bibles. These are John 1:1-3 and 14; Colossians 1:15-16; and Hebrews 1:1-3"

He waited until each one had found the opening chapter of the gospel of John. Once they had read the verses he had mentioned, they moved on to Colossians and then Hebrews. Then Philip said, "So, if Jesus Christ is the Creator, where then, do the Father and Holy Spirit come in?

"Let's return to Genesis, chapter one. In verse two, we see, quite plainly stated,*...the Spirit of God was hovering over the waters...*Therefore, the Holy Spirit was directly involved. Now, what about the Father?"

Both James and Andrea looked at him, but shook their heads slowly.

"Perhaps, James and Andrea," said Philip, "the following 'explanation' might be helpful. I see Father God as the *Ideas Person;* we know that Jesus is called the *Word* or expression of God, remember, we just read that, so when Jesus, who is always perfectly in tune with His Father, *speaks the word,* He expresses God's thoughts and will. That makes sense, doesn't it?"

They nodded.

"Well then," Philip continued, "the Holy Spirit is the one who *expresses the energy* to accomplish their jointly agreed purpose! I say this, because he is connected to *power* in the Bible—the New Testament Greek uses the word *dunamis,* dynamite power, as the imagery here. Does this help?

"Please just interrupt with a question..." he said, looking at James and Andrea again. "So, *Elohim* created—the Hebrew word is *bara*—which means to create out of nothing, something only God can do. *He made everything out of nothing!*

"The third thing we need to see is that the words 'heavens and the earth' come from a combination of Hebrew words. These are *hashamayim we ha'erets,* and this means the totality of the entire universe, all the galaxies, planets, dust, gas, stars, black holes and everything. Okay, let's stop there and discuss!"

"No problems, so far," replied James, "I must say, though, that I am running everything through my 'astronomy grid' so to speak, and no hiccups yet. How about you, hon?" he asked Andrea.

She looked excited. "This is *great stuff,* Philip!" she said, enthusiastically. "Let's keep going!"

"All right," said Philip, and he cleared his throat. "Notice that 'heavens' is plural, while 'earth' is singular. The Bible informs us that there are at least three heavens. We read elsewhere that God lives in the 'third' or highest heaven. It appears from scripture that the first heaven is a physical place, the sky, where the birds fly, or where the stars are. That leaves a 'second heaven', which is the spiritual dimension around planet earth, or wherever humans are. The Bible sometimes refers to the second heaven as the *heavenly places*. We could go and look up those passages in the Bible, but take my word for it at present. We can refer to them later if you like.

"Now, I want to show you the ten steps of creation in the chronology given to us in Genesis chapter one. The first step, we have already looked at. It was the *initiation event,* some astronomers call it the 'inflationary primordial explosion,' or 'Hot Big Bang.'

"Now for step two, given in verses 2-5: Let's read these first," and they did. Then he continued. "Let me explain: Exercising great selectivity, *Elohim* sent His Holy Spirit to one of the millions of galaxies that he had allowed to form over billions of years as we measure time on the Earth—and remember, for God, time does not really matter. Then he selected one tiny planet, called Earth, of one of the stars which is our Sun, and he descended through the choking darkness to the watery surface. Using enormous energy and power he cleared the opaque atmosphere of that planet from clouds of gas and dust, so that periods of daylight and darkness (night) could be distinguished. We read, *'Let there be light,'* that's what that's all about. The result was a change in Earth's atmosphere from opaque to *translucent.* Translucent is not clear, or transparent, but like frosted glass on a bathroom window. It was something like the daylight on a heavily overcast day. God wanted light on that planet, so that He could start to brood life!

"You may be interested to know that scientists have identified more than forty characteristics of the Sun and planet Earth that are so finely tuned, that any variation of only tiny amounts, would prevent life existing. In fact they have calculated that the chances are infinitesimal, *one chance in a quintillion*, that any other planet with such favourable conditions for life even exists!

Philip paused and Andrea waved a hand, "So, you are saying that there are no other planets in the entire universe?"

"Oh no!" replied Philip. "There are probably millions of planets in the universe. What I am telling you is that astronomers, who believe that they have seen the formation of planets around the birth of new stars, have said that the conditions of young planets is just like the Bible describes it in Genesis verse two—*formless and void*—the surface covered with swirling gases and interplanetary debris. They have also calculated that *the chances* are that there is no other planet in the entire universe with the unique characteristic that planet Earth has!"

"Why is that? Do you mind, Philip, explaining that again?" asked Andrea.

Philip looked up. "Because so many factors have been discovered on planet earth that, were they altered, even by minute amounts, life could not exist. Here's one example: Did you know that a change in the distance of the earth from the sun as small as two percent, would rid the planet of all life?"

Andrea shook her head. "Why...how is that?" she asked.

"If the earth was just two percent closer to the sun, it would be so hot on the planet that all water would evaporate and dissipate into the atmosphere. On the other hand, if the earth were two percent further away fro the sun, all liquid water would freeze. There would be run away freezing, permanent ice-age!"

Andrea nodded. "So it is all about probabilities, is it?"

"Yes," said Philip, "It *is* from a scientific perspective, and that's all I'm saying at present. Shall we carry on?"

They both nodded.

"Now, that uniqueness of our planet, isn't that amazing?" asked Philip. "James, you are very quiet. How are you finding this?"

"I'm listening," he said, "and I'm enjoying it. Of course, like I said, having studied astronomy, I run everything I hear through a sort of sieve, to see if it holds true. So far, no problems, and, it is making a lot of sense."

"Good," said Philip. "Now I want to tell you something *very* important. If you really get a hold of the next thing I say, many, many problems you have, or might have, with the Genesis account of creation will vanish. It is very important that you grasp the fact that from Genesis 1 verse 2, onwards, the perspective is NOT from outer space, but from the *surface of the planet-starting from the surface of the oceans.* That's why I read about the Holy Spirit going to the watery surface of the planet in her primordial days, and saying, 'Let there be light,' remember?

"This explains the complete darkness on proto-planet Earth and the conditions which could not support life—expressed clearly in verse 2—*formless and void,* literally a waste and emptiness, completely uninhabitable. Do you get that?"

"I think I am starting to see something I never saw before," said

James, slowly. "That perspective sets the stage for verse three, doesn't it? Now, I'm getting a whole new handle on this story..."

"Yes, you are absolutely right, James. The fact that verse two informs us that the Holy Spirit of God was on the surface of the primordial oceans of Planet Earth, allows us to understand verse three correctly. Do you follow, Andrea? You see, the Hot Big Bang, produced light, lots of it! Light did not come into being for the first time when God spoke in verse three. Light was already in existence. But, no light had penetrated the thick clouds of dust, gases, and interplanetary debris that was choking Earth's atmosphere in the early days of her existence.

"That is why we need to read verse two carefully, in fact, why we need to read any part of the Bible carefully, to see what it *really* says! Verse two says the Spirit of God was moving, or hovering, or brooding—all three translations of the Hebrew are permissible—and together they shed some important light on the subject, excuse the pun! So, what was He doing on the surface of the oceans? He was exerting enormous energy. The picture is like a gigantic helicopter, hovering, and clearing the atmosphere! God the Holy Spirit was clearing the opaque atmosphere to allow light to get through to the surface of the planet. He was also doing something else. He was brooding life in the oceans! That is where life started.

"All this, sets the stage for those first recorded words from God: *Let there be light.* Then the epoch closes with the statement: *And there was evening and there was morning, one day."*

"I have a question for you, Philip," said James. "When do you believe that God initiated things? I mean, you know, how long ago was the Hot Big Bang, and when was Planet Earth formed? Do you have a view on those things?"

"Well, I do have a view," said Philip, "and I will share it with you, but it is simply *my* view. There are many who might differ with me about these things. I believe that the scientific evidence reveals that the Hot Big Bang occurred about fifteen billion years ago—and *that* number is the average of four or five different measurements, I am told. Our star, the sun, is about four and a half billion years old, and the planets formed at the same time. The moon is younger, from measurements made on rocks the astronauts brought back to Earth, and seems to have been an intrusion into the solar system, *a miracle moon* in many respects. I also understand that the Hot Big Bang is no longer disputed among top level scientists."

James was looking closely at Philip. "Man! You have an incredible grasp of this stuff," he exclaimed. "Where, how, did you get all this information?"

"I have always been interested in origins, so I have read much on the subject. Some of what is in print is garbage, I find you have to pick through it all carefully…Now, I feel like a cup of tea, how about you two?"

Andrea jumped up. "Let me get it," she said, "I need to go down to the cottage, myself." And she hurried off.

"Philip, could you help me? I also need to go to the bathroom," said Barker.

"Sure," said Philip, and carefully, he helped James off the bed, and held him as he hopped to the washroom.

Philip went through to see how Dorothy was doing, and found her busy examining a young fisherman from the village. "A nasty cut, this," she remarked, seeing Philip arrive. "But not fatal! He managed to slice himself quite deeply with a machete when he was down at the beach. But, disinfected and stitched up, it will heal."

"How about some tea, love?" Philip asked.

"Best idea I've come across all morning," Dorothy replied. "I'll come and join you all in the hospital room when I'm finished here."

Later, as they sipped tea together, Dorothy turned to Andrea. "So, how are you getting on with Genesis chapter one?"

"Oh, I'm loving it!" said Andrea. "Philip has made it sound so *real!* For the first time, I am starting to get a clearer picture of how creation started. I still have many questions, about evolution and stuff, but I'm sure we will get around to those later."

"How about you, James?" Dorothy turned to face him as he lay propped up on the bed.

"Same thing," he replied. "Things are falling into place for me, too. I am very impressed with Philip's grasp of scientific matters. I thought he was an accountant!"

Dorothy chuckled. "This wonderful husband of mine is much more than an accountant," she said.

21

When Dorothy had gone back to her medical duties, Philip said, "James, Andrea, can you take any more of this today? We can continue tomorrow, if you want to reflect on what we've looked at already."

"Let's go on," they both said in unison, and laughed.

"Okay, then. Let's look at verses four and five. The thing I want to focus on in these verses is the word 'day.' Notice it says, *And there was evening and there was morning, one day.* The Hebrew word *yom,* translated 'day' here, appears throughout the Old Testament, and is used to describe any period of time varying from a specified hour of a day, that's in 1 Kings, 18:36; to about twelve hours of daylight, that's in Numbers 11:32. The same word is used for a period of thirty-eight years in Deuteronomy 2:14; for all the years of the reign of a king in 2 Samuel 2:11; and to the lifetime of an individual, as is written in Ezra 9:7"

Philip waited and encouraged James and Andrea to look up each reference that he had mentioned. Then he continued. "Furthermore the same word, *yom,* refers to an enormous epoch of billions of years in Genesis 2:4. One thing is certain: what is NOT meant by "day" *is a period of 24 hours!* There are excellent reasons for this: firstly, the unusual sentence construction, literally, *and was evening and was morning day X*, alerts us to the fact that a period of a single rotation of the planet is not the meaning here. Secondly, scientists also know that in her youth, the rotation of the earth was much faster than at present-a day being only about 8 hours!"

Philip paused here and all three remained silent for a few minutes. Barker in particular, seemed deep in thought. Then he spoke up.

"You know, Philip, what strikes me is the fact that the first day is announced only after the clearing of the opaque atmosphere in verse 5. I think that is telling us something."

"What are you seeing, James?' asked Philip.

"Well," replied Barker, "I think this strongly suggests that God's 'day' is very different from ours. You said earlier, Philip, that God lives outside of Earth time. So, maybe the perspective is from Earth's *spatially*, but not from the time as we measure it in days now, because as you mentioned, too, planet Earth's rotation was much faster initially. So, a day back then was only about a third as long as one is now."

"Right," said Philip, "we also see in the Bible, that the 'seventh day' has not been closed out, like all the others have been, and, so far, is thousands of years long! That, in itself, tells us something, don't you think? No, the 'days' mentioned in Genesis chapter one, cannot be taken to mean twenty-four-hour periods. They are meant to imply that God created everything in an orderly sequence which took place over billions of years.

"You see," continued Philip, "we need to remember that God invented science! God established all scientific laws, and generally speaking, He abides by the laws he made. For God, who lives in a different realm of existence to us—a timeless eternity really—time as we measure it is not the same to Him. I mean it is, but it isn't. Do you follow?"

"I do," answered James, "but, if God took billions of years to create things, because time doesn't bother Him since He lives outside of time, then doesn't this great time allow for evolution to have brought forth life on the earth? Did God put evolution in place as the mechanism of generating and evolving all the different life forms?"

"No," said Philip. "I do not believe that, not for one minute! And nor do I believe that the Bible allows for that. Furthermore, I understand that many distinguished scientists, and not all of them Christians by the way, have refuted the theory of macro-evolution in no uncertain terms. There is simply no decent evidence to support the theory of macro-evolution. Indeed, all the evidence points to special creation, and embarrassingly so for evolutionists, I might add! However, micro-evolution, which is adaptations in a species over time, you know, the changes they make to successfully cope with changes in their environment, *is an established scientific fact.* And, I do not see any argument between the Bible and micro-evolution."

"I would like to discuss that with you, perhaps at some later stage," said Barker, and Kitson nodded.

"Shall I continue?" he inquired.

"Please do," said Andrea, and Barker looked at her in surprise.

"I'm game, too," he said, "Hey honey, are you *getting all this stuff?"*

"Oh, *yabetcha*!" Andrea replied, "I'm lapping this up!"

"What I'm going to suggest then," said Philip, "is that I simply point out the remaining steps in creation from Genesis 1.

"Step three is found in verses 6-8. It concerns the formation of a stable water cycle, and took place over another enormous epoch of time called the 'second day.' Step four is covered in verses 9 and 10; and step five in verses 11-13. Have you noted those?"

Both Barker and Andrea nodded in unison, so Philip continued.

"Step six is interesting. It is covered in verses 14-19, and at first sight appears to contradict some of the things we talked about in step one. Many people stumble over this verse, and have to invent all sorts of theories to explain a solar system without the Sun etcetera. They see that God made the Sun on the fourth day, and *BOOM*, that mucks everything up for them. But finding out what certain Hebrew words mean, solves the problem. Notice that it says in verse 16 that God *made* the sun and the moon, and the stars. It does not say that he *created* them. The Hebrew word translated as 'made' is *asah,* and it means to bring forth, to accomplish to completeness, and to celebrate the appearance of something already there!"

Andrea raised her hand. "Whoa, Philip," she cried, "I would *never* have been able to figure that out by myself. I'm not a Hebrew scholar!"

Philip chuckled. "Nor am I, dear," he said. "But that is why we all learn from teachers, and from other researchers, right? And, there are study aids available which help you to understand the meaning of Hebrew and Greek words that were used in the original writing of the Bible. You could do just the same research that I have done to find out what the Bible actually says. The problem is, that too many people do *not* do the necessary research, and then when they are given either silly or fanciful explanations, they are unable to refute them, or worse, they just swallow what they are told."

"Hey, Philip," broke in James, "This is tying things up so well! You know," he went on, "we should have been taught this at school, and college, and university. Then all the antagonism toward the Bible would not exist."

Philip chuckled again. "I wish that were true, James," he said. "But the truth is that rebellious and sinful humans would still look for ways to discredit the Bible. And there are several reasons for that. One is that fallen man does not want to face God. Humans do not want to be accountable for their behaviour that they know deep down is wrong. Another reason concerns God's enemy, Satan. He does all he can to keep humans from finding the truth!"

James and Andrea were quiet for a long moment. Then Philip said, "I am going to go just a little further, and give you the other steps. We've covered a huge amount of ground this morning, and I don't want to blow your minds. Okay? Steps seven and eight are dealt with in verses 20-23. This was when God created the *nephesh,* that's the Hebrew word for creatures, and means soulish animals of every kind, one's with mind, will and emotions.

"Step nine is found in verses 24 and 25, and these *nephesh* are the creatures that relate closely to human beings such as dogs, horses and cats. As far as I can tell, steps one to nine line up with the findings of most biologists, chemists, physicists, geologists, and astronomers. I am not going to go into step ten, today. There are so many things to that step, and it is so *personal*—it involves us human beings—that we will need to spend a lot of time on that step."

With that, Philip closed his Bible and stood up. "Ponder these things," he said, "Think over what we have looked at together this morning. It has been a lot to digest. Perhaps we can discuss them tomorrow or another day." Then he left James and Andrea and walked out into the sunshine.

22

The following day, when Andrea awoke, she found that Philip had gone off to the Islanders' village to respond to Farulap's invitation to him to 'come and explain some things.' His note to her and James, which she found on the breakfast table, said that he expected to be back by about noon.

She carried breakfast up to James and sat eating with him. It was simple fare; granola cereal and some sliced mangoes. After they had eaten, Andrea poured the coffee and took a cup through to Dorothy, who was treating a sick woman. She left the coffee on Dorothy's desk, and returned to James' room.

"Have you read the rest of chapter one?" asked James.

"Yes," I have, she replied, "I read the whole chapter through again yesterday afternoon, and it makes so much more sense to me now. Actually, to be honest, I last read it, or had it read to me, in Sunday school."

"Yeah, ditto. You know, honey, all I can remember about Genesis, and the Bible in general, is the ridicule that was thrown around about it all. And I was no saint in that regard, myself. Once I had gotten into astronomy, that was *it,* concerning the Bible, and of course concerning Christianity, too. My opinion was, *'if the first page of the Bible is wrong, why bother to turn to the second page or the rest of the book.'"*

"I know what you mean. We used to think in much the same way when I was at school and also later, at college. Some of our teachers were the worst offenders."

"Oh, tell me about it!" exclaimed James. "Were they ever! Some of those profs at university were so arrogant, and ridiculed the Bible just to sound and look 'cool.' I would love to go back and talk with a few of them now, but of course, I'm being arrogant myself, when I say that, because I was in their space until very recently."

"Did you come up with any questions, when you read the rest of the chapter?" asked Andrea.

"Yeah," said James. "I guess I wondered where the dinosaurs were, or rather weren't. And the insects."

"Oh, aren't the insects mentioned in verse 24, and at the end of verse 26?"

"You mean the 'creeping things?" Well, maybe, but Philip said that the creatures God made in step nine, were animals that related closely with humans. So I didn't think that means insects. But, *there's* a question or two for Philip. Is he coming up this morning?"

"Oh, no, I forgot to tell you. He was called away to the Islanders' village and left a note for us saying he would only be back at noon."

"It's funny that, isn't it? I mean, not that he hasn't come to us, but how he waits to be invited by the Islanders. He told me once that he only teaches and preaches if he is asked to. That's neat, hey? *Only when he's invited.* That's when people have ears to hear, he said."

"How's your leg feeling? Has the pain gone completely?"

"Yes, completely," said Barker. "Unless, of course, I twist it or bump it or do something stupid. What about your arm?"

Andrea held up her arm and twisted it inside the cast. "Absolutely fine. No pain whatsoever. Dorothy looked at it last night, and seemed pleased with it."

"Darling," said James, softly, "won't you come a little closer, right here," he indicated the side of the bed near where he was sitting.

"Is it safe?" asked Andrea in an exaggerated whisper. "I mean, with you having been confined to this room all this time an' all, will it be safe for me to approach you?"

Barker grinned, and made a grab at her, but missed as she danced out of reach.

"Oh boy!" she said, "I can see it is not safe!"

Barker slumped over on his side, facing her. An awful groan came out of his mouth, and he screwed up his face as if in great pain. He put both hands down and held the cast on his injured leg.

"Honey!" cried Andrea in alarm, "What have you done to yourself?" And she ran to him.

Quick as a flash he grabbed her, and pulled her down for a kiss. She softened and they smooched for a moment. She was lying in his arms at his side, and about to comment about him 'crying wolf' when Dorothy spoke from the doorway. "If you would rather I returned later..."

Andrea leapt off the bed, blushing furiously, and Barker grinned at Dorothy.

Before Dorothy could speak again, Andrea cried out, "You saved me, Dorothy! This beast of a man enticed me within his reach and I was helpless for a while."

It was Dorothy's turn to keep up the little façade. "Well!" she said, "I have learned a new definition of 'helpless', then! And, as for you, young man, you must be feeling *so* much better."

She came in with a tray of fresh tea, and pulled up a chair.

"I suppose your next question, James Barker, is going to be something like this: 'Dr Kitson.... When can I get up and move around? I *really want to go down to my boat.*' Am I right?"

"You are not only a doctor," said Barker, "But I can see that you are a psychiatrist, a clairvoyant, a mind-reader, and a woman!"

Dorothy chuckled. "Yes," she said. "I have to be all of those things in this profession-except the clairvoyant bit—I don't want to be into that sort of thing.... Is there any pain at all?"

"None," he said. "No, there is no pain as such. Just a little, sort of, tenderness, actually."

"Well," she replied, "tomorrow. I will get Philip to dig out the crutches—we have some, you know—and we will adjust them to your size. You can move around a little, but no weight on it for quite a while, yet."

Philip came bouncing in shortly after two that afternoon. He had spent several hours teaching the villagers and answering questions. "It's so good," he said, "not having to help people unlearn all the non-Biblical junk that has become status quo and tradition in western churchianity. I am delighting in the experience of being a part of an *indigenous church.* Anyway, have you two read chapter one, and did you encounter any stumbling blocks?"

"No stumbling blocks," said James, "but I have a question or two. And I think Andrea might have, also."

"Fire away," said Philip as he pulled up a chair.

"I just wondered about the dinosaurs, and also that God simply spoke, and things happened."

"And I wondered where the insects were, that's all," piped up Andrea.

Philip opened his Bible. "We need to see an amazing thing about this creation account. Firstly, Moses, who wrote it down under the inspiration of the Holy Spirit, lived *three thousand four hundred years ago.* The whole story is given in thirty one verses which spell out the ten steps. *Just think about that.* He could *never* have guessed the right steps, *and* their correct sequence. The chances are remote.

"Secondly, God chose not to give every little detail. Events like life-destroying asteroid collisions, ice-ages, primordial floods, and dinosaurs are not there. But what *is* there, is the most credible and accurate creation account among those of all the religions' in the world. So, insects? I suppose the 'creeping things' might have sounded to you like insects? Well, I believe that insects are not mentioned, specifically. I think that the *nephesh* refers to cattle, sheep, horses, camels and goats, animals that were a help to humans. The creeping things, I believe are short legged animals like dogs and cats and rabbits, again, creatures that relate to humans.

"And about God simply speaking things into being, James: Firstly, remember that it is God at work, and He chose to do it that way. Secondly, the Bible informs us there is the power of life and death in the tongue, and that harshly spoken words are like the thrusting of a sword, they hurt, and do damage. Jesus' name is the *Word of God*. Spoken words are very important to God. Jesus often simply spoke healing and it happened. The words carried his power. That's a partial answer at least, James. Shall we continue?"

"Yes, I'm looking forward to it," said James, and Andrea nodded in agreement.

"Okay. Let's look at step ten, then. This is covered in verses 26-31. You see, after all the rest of the creating work, the time finally came for *Elohim* to make His ultimate creature-the one in which He would place a *spirit*. We read in verses 26 and 27, that the Father, Son and Holy Spirit had a discussion among themselves about creating humans in their image and likeness.

"Now Jesus told us that God is a *spirit*, and if we wish to worship Him, that is, to connect with Him, we can only do so with our human spirits. Therefore, to be made in his image and likeness, to be like Him, that is, *triune*, humans must themselves possess a spirit, a soul and a body. That is, a triune nature. God is triune, and we humans, being made in His image, are also triune. Okay. We will learn how this came about in Genesis chapter two. Are you following this, so far, James and Andrea? No problems?"

"Yeah..." said James, slowly, "but I need some clarification about the spirit and soul bit. Aren't those two things the same, really?"

"No, they are not the same," said Philip. "Both the Old and New Testaments use words for the soul which mean the mind or will or emotions or some combination of those faculties. We are thinking, decision-making and feeling beings. But our spirit is the eternal part of us which connects with God, who *is spirit*, remember. In the book of Hebrews, we read that the word of God is sharper than any two edged sword, able to separate the soul from the spirit.

"Now it is only logical, isn't it, that if the spirit and the soul can be divided, then they are not one and the same thing? No, the Bible says clearly that humans are triune, being spirit, soul, and body, and that each part is distinct."

"Hmm..." mused Barker, "interesting...I've always thought that Aristotle had it right when he taught that man is body and soul, and the soul is that part of man that is spiritual, or something along those lines. I see that the soul is our personality, so to speak. But, I still don't quite get the distinction between the spirit and the soul."

"Yes, Philip," chipped in Andrea, "could you spell that out a bit more for us?"

"Okay," replied Philip. "let me see...let's look at Genesis chapter two and verse seven, to start with."

They found the place and read the verse together: *Then the LORD God formed man of the dust of the ground, and breathed into his nostrils the breath of life; and man became a living soul.*

Philip continued, "I want you to notice here that God *formed* the body of man. He did not *create* it, He formed it. 'Formed' is from the Hebrew word *yatsar,* which means to fashion out of existing material. You and I can 'yatsar' things, we can form things. If you see a wooden table, you are seeing the result of a person who fashioned that table out of a tree! The person took existing material, the tree, and formed it into something he wanted, something very different in appearance. You and I, Andrea, watched James *yatsar* some fibreglass and resin into a patch that covered a hole on the stern of your boat.

"Now, we are even told in verse seven what the existing material is, from which God formed man. He used the *dust* of the *ground.* The Hebrew word for ground here is *adamah,* from which the body of Adam was formed. *Adamah* means 'red earth.' Our bodies are terrestrial, containing many of the elements found on planet earth. So, our body is one part of our triune nature.

"Then, verse seven goes on to inform us that God breathed the *breath of life* into the nostrils of the man's body that He had formed out of red earth. The words *breath of life* are from the Hebrew, *ruach,* the same word for spirit. So, when the *ruach,* or spirit entered the body, something else came into being—man became a living soul. The word soul, also translated 'being' in some Bibles, is from *nephesh,* the Hebrew word also used for 'creatures' in Genesis one. Do you remember it?"

They nodded.

"So, we humans are triune, we are composed of spirit, soul, and body," said Philip, "and once you get hold of *that,* many things about the Bible, about God, and about the spiritual world become clear!"

"This is marvellous, Philip," said Andrea. "I want to go over all the notes I scribbled down, and really get a firm hold on it all."

"Yes, so do I," said James. "This is great stuff...and there is a lot to think about...I want to ponder the spirit-soul bit a bit longer."

"Yes," replied Philip, "think about it for a while, and maybe we can discuss it tomorrow. For the present, I think we should just complete Genesis chapter one, if you are game?"

"All right," said Andrea, "I'm game...how about you, James?"

"Sure," he replied.

"Okay," said Philip. "Chapter one closes with instructions on a vegetarian diet for both humans and animals, but it is important to realize that *death* must occur in the eating and digestion of living plant matter. In fact, digestion is *work,* involving the Second Law of Thermodynamics, the law of entropy? You remember that one? It states that systems degrade to lower and lower levels of energy, order, complexity and information. Things are winding down.

"Consider, too, the testimony of billions of fossils throughout geological history. The existence of limestone, marble, coal, gas, oil, kerogen, peat, coral reefs, and guano deposits in great abundance on Earth, tells us of millions of generations of past *life and death*, through which means the Creator carefully provided for us, the creature made in His image and likeness! It is through His loving care that we have our fuel and other needs met so marvellously today. When ever you drove your car, James, or started the diesel engine on your boat, you were only able to do so because of the death of millions of living things over millions of years. Think about that! So, there, that's it. That is what Genesis chapter one is about!"

Philip closed his Bible and looked at James and Andrea. It was Barker who spoke first.

"Wow," he breathed, "what a difference! *Man,*" he spoke more animatedly, "*what a difference! If I had only been taught this years ago...*"

23

The next morning, Dorothy and Philip surprised James by arriving early at his bedside with formidable looking equipment. "We are going to change your cast," she said, and without further ado, they went to work. This was a painless procedure, and when Andrea entered shortly after they had finished removing the old cast, Dorothy immediately commissioned her to bathe James leg down with warm, soapy water. Once the washing and drying was done, Dorothy and Philip went to work applying a new cast. "There is no walking brace in this cast," said Dorothy. "So, that means no weight on the leg, okay?"

Philip handed James a pair of crutches, and said, with a grin, "Breakfast will be served in the cottage!"

They helped him to get off the bed and adjust the crutches to fit his body height and length of arms. Then he went down the pathway to the cottage and was surprised at the strain it took to move such a short distance.

Breakfast was a grand affair that morning. Philip had baked a fresh loaf of bread from scratch, and with some help from Dorothy, he had fried up a large platter of scrambled eggs, bacon, potato chips from a packet, and egg-plant from his garden. Andrea had sliced up some canned pears and fresh mangoes as the starter, and there was bitter orange marmalade and sweet strawberry jam for the bread or toast available afterwards with their tea. Before they began the meal, Philip and Dorothy held hands and reached out to include James and Andrea. Without explanation, Philip simply spoke quietly. "*Father God, Dorothy, Andrea and I want to thank you for the healing that is taking place in James' leg, and Andrea's arm. This is the day that You have made, and we choose to rejoice and be glad in it. Thank You for this food. Amen*"

Then everyone tucked in to the feast before them. After breakfast, Dorothy suggested they all sit out on the front lawn. There were four chairs there, and Philip brought a small stool and a pillow for James to rest his leg on. It was another beautiful morning, and the sea was sparkling as the sunshine reflected off the ripples made by a soft breeze. After a short silence, James spoke.

"Philip, Dorothy," he said, "I want to discuss something with you. Is that okay?" He had taken Andrea's hand as he spoke.

"What is it you wish to know, James?" asked Philip.

"Last night I did not sleep very much. I lay in bed and thought about all the things you had taught us during the afternoon. Actually, I found myself totally at peace with the *sense it all made,* but in a turmoil over a strange effect it was having inside of me." He was silent for a long moment, before continuing.

"I don't really know what is going on..." his voice was husky, and Andrea looked at him, closely. "But, I feel sort of *bad,* you know, about things. About my selfishness, my arrogance, my neglecting of—er—well—er—*stuff, sin, in my life! It's just below the surface*...I felt, last night you know, that God was getting my attention. It was the strangest thing, really. I felt he was saying to me, *'James, where are you?'* And, it *was* the strangest thing....I couldn't answer...I was trying to hide...but I knew all the time he was looking for me..." James had let go of Andrea's hand, and wiped his cheeks. He was trying as hard as he knew how, to control his emotions.

Philip leaned over toward him, and spoke softly. "James, God has been trying to get your attention. He loves you. You can be free of your burdens, cleansed from your sin. That's why Jesus died. Just ask God now, to forgive you."

There was silence for a minute or two. Then James closed his eyes.

"God," he choked out, "Please forgive me...for all the sin and junk in my life!"

Philip spoke again. "James, do you believe that Jesus Christ was God in human flesh?"

"Yes, I do!" spluttered Barker.

"Tell Him you trust Him as your Lord and Saviour."

"I do... Lord Jesus... Thank You..."

Dorothy and Philip moved over to where James was speaking, and they each placed their hands on him.

"Thank You, Lord Jesus, for giving us a new brother and citizen in Your Kingdom. Bless him. Protect him. Keep him from the evil one."

James heard, but was not sure who had spoken. He let his tears fall unashamedly to the grass. There was a long period of silence on the lawn in front of the Kitson's little cottage after that. Eventually, James' tears stopped flowing and he sat leaning back in his chair with his eyes closed.

Andrea stood up, and went and knelt between Philip and Dorothy's chairs. She took each one by the hand. She, too, was close to tears.

"Philip, Dorothy," she said. I want to pray those prayers of confession, too."

It was Philip who spoke first.

"Dear," he said, "I believe that you are already a child of God. But, if saying the prayers will confirm something in your heart, we will be glad to hear them."

Andrea thanked Christ for His sacrifice on her behalf. She confessed Him as Lord and said that she believed He had risen from the dead. Then she stood up with Philip and Dorothy, and all three held on to each other.

Then, Philip prayed: *"Father, thank You for the privilege of serving You! Thank You for the plan You have for James' and Andrea' lives. May they lead thousands of lost people back into Your Kingdom."* And Dorothy's *Amen,* echoed his.

The four of them sat quietly together for a long time, wrapped in their own thoughts. Finally, it was Barker who broke the silence.

"Philip, Dorothy, I want to thank you for all you have done for us, for Andrea and for me. You have been amazingly kind and hospitable. And for all the medical treatment...thank you so much!"

He paused for a while before continuing. "It's strange, it's a funny feeling I have, sort of like *feeling lighter,* as though a huge load has dropped off my back and from my insides!"

Philip smiled at him. "James," he said softly, "something has indeed dropped off you! It was a heavy load of guilt and sin—the *stuff* you were referring to earlier. It has gone. God has thrown it into the depths of the sea. He has cleansed you with the Blood of Christ. That is the marvellous thing about salvation. No other religion can come close to dealing with the human sin problem, and they all carry guilt in one form or another. But Christ, God in human flesh, has dealt with the human sin problem. *That is what you are feeling, and what a blessing it is."*

Barker looked down at the grass beneath his feet. Then he looked up and asked, "Do you mind if we stay on a little longer? With you two, I mean, here on Truk Island?" Then he looked at Andrea whose eyes were shining.

"Darling," he said, reaching out and taking hold of her hand, "Before Philip and Dorothy as witnesses, I ask you...will you marry me?"

"Oh yes!" she said huskily. "Yes, yes, I will!"

And turning to Philip, he said, looking him squarely in the eyes, "Philip, will you marry us?"

"I would be honoured!" was the reply they both heard…

Epilogue

Three weeks later James Barker and Andrea Jensen were married. Philip Kitson led them through a simple but profound ceremony on the lawn in front of the cottage. The witnesses present included Dorothy, both sets of parents, and James' sister, Ruth. Finances for the five air-fares had mysteriously arrived at their homes in Victoria, together with a formal invitation to attend and spend a week on Truk Island.

The newly married couple remained with the Kitsons on Big Truk, and received much Bible teaching from Philip. One year after their marriage, they sailed the fully repaired Robson to a nearby island to serve as missionaries in that place.

Farulap grew in both zeal and knowledge of God and His Word. Not content with simply guiding the church in his village, he regularly sailed a catamaran to neighbouring islands and evangelised hundreds of Islanders over the following ten years.

Philip and Dorothy Kitson continued their work on Big Truk, and met monthly with the Barkers for fellowship.

One month after the Great White had attacked James' boat for the second time, the fishermen from Truk discovered its partially eaten carcass lying on the beach on Little Truk Island. Despite the missing flesh, the ruptured stomach of the shark was clearly visible.

These injuries had been caused by the broken ends of the stern guard rails on *Skipping Stone,* and told the story. Mortally injured in that attack, the Great White had suffered and slowly died not far from the place where it had killed and eaten five Islanders.